Spring with the Moodys

by Sarah Maxwell

illustrated by Tilaundia Hale

CCI Communication Concepts, Inc.

Spring with the Moodys

Ordering information:

Titus2, Inc.
1504 Santa Fe Street
Leavenworth, Kansas 66048
Phone: (913) 772-0392
Web site: www.Titus2.com

Published by:

Communication Concepts, Inc.
Web site: www.we-communicate.com

ACKNOWLEDGMENTS

Scripture taken from the HOLY BIBLE, KING JAMES VER-SION.

ISBN 978-0-9771420-6-4

Printed in the United States of America.

1 2 3 4

This book was created in Microsoft Word. QuarkXPress 6.5 and Adobe Photoshop were used for layout and design. All computers were Windows-based systems running Windows XP/2000.

Christopher Maxwell designed the cover, and Sarah Maxwell designed the interior of this book. Tilaundia Hale drew the illustrations.

This book is dedicated to:

Susannah Joy Maxwell

Near the end of this book project, in swept the biggest trial of our lives. My precious little long-awaited niece, Susannah Joy, was born March 21st, 2007, to Nathan and Melanie. She only lived a few days, and on March 24th, 2007, she slipped into the arms of our Lord and Savior.

"For the Lamb which is in the midst of the throne shall feed them, and shall lead them unto living fountains of waters: and God shall wipe away all tears from their eyes" (Revelation 7:17).

Contents

Preface

I am grateful to my family for all the help they have been with this book. Without them, *Spring with the Moodys* would not have been completed! You will even see characteristics of my family members along with some of our daily life and experiences.

After writing *Winter with the Moodys,* I had ideas for *Spring with the Moodys.* As I worked through the outline, wrote the book, and then edited, Jesus gave me fresh direction all the way.

My desire is that the Moody Family Series would be used to encourage families to draw closer to Jesus and to each other. I want to hold up a model for children that would cause them to choose to be loving, helpful, kind, and considerate—more like Jesus. I have endeavored to present the gospel of salvation to each child reading this book. I hope to cause my readers to want to spend time in the Word and in prayer every day. While the Moody family may seem like a perfect family, they are the picture of a family that Scripture sets before us. May we all strive to be a part of that kind of family.

I'm grateful to Tilaundia for doing the illustrations for the book. I know younger readers especially enjoy them!

If you notice the small, white lilies on the four corners of the book cover, they have a very special significance. As noted in the dedication, my little niece, Susannah Joy, was born and went to be with Jesus when this book was in the final stages. Susannah's name means lily. We needed a flower to go in each corner of the book, and Anna, my sweet sister, had the idea to use a lily. It seemed perfect! We were at the last minute timing-wise, but we contacted some friends whose daughter is an artist. She graciously agreed to do the drawing, and the lily came out very well! Thank you, Abi!

Thank you again to the Jackson family who allowed us to use their dog, Lady, on the *Autumn, Winter,* and *Spring* book covers. Near the end of this project, two moms of twins graciously agreed to read the book to make sure my details were accurate and also to provide "back cover" comments. Their feedback was appreciated! Two other families read the book and submitted "back cover" comments.

May Jesus Christ draw you and your family closer to Him.

Joyfully His,

Sarah Maxwell

Meet the Characters

Mr. Moody—Dad (Jim) is the happy father of six children. He works at a bank. When he has fulfilled his duties at work, his preferred place is at home, spending time with his family. His heart's desire is to be a man of God and the spiritual leader of his family.

Mrs. Moody—Mom (Emily) is a homeschooling, stay-at-home mom. She dearly loves being a helpmeet to her husband and mother to her six children.

Max—Max (Maxwell) turns twelve in this book and enjoys being the oldest child. Max has a heart for the Lord and wants to please Him.

Mollie—Mollie, ten, is a happy young lady. She loves Jesus and looks for ways to bless others.

Mitch—Mitch (Mitchell), nine, tends to have a unique suggestion or comment for the situation at hand. He makes his time in God's Word a priority each day.

Maddie—Four-year-old Madelynn, affectionately known as Maddie, is no longer the youngest of the Moody family. Her cute comments and view of life add a spark to the Moody household.

Twins—You'll meet the Moody twins in this book.

Grandpa and Grandma—James and Martha are Dad's parents, and both recently accepted the Lord as their Savior.

Grandma Clifton—Mrs. Clifton is an elderly widow whom the Moodys have helped and also the owner of Honey, a golden retriever.

Mrs. Maud Bagwell—Mrs. Bagwell lives up the road from the Moodys, and she has a pet rat named Snickers.

Mr. Delome—Mr. Delome is the Moodys' neighbor who lives across the street.

National Pastor—The Moodys support a national pastor in Zambia. If you would like to know more about national pastors and how you may support them, visit this site: www.FamiliesforJesus.com/pastors

Mr. and Mrs. Russell—They are friends of the Moody family and owners of Peaches, the cat, whom the Moody children pet-sat for a little while over the summer.

Background

The Moody family lives in a city called Sunflower, nestled among the rolling hills of eastern Kansas. They have been homeschooling since Max was in preschool. Even though Dad currently works at a bank, his desire is that he might someday have a business with his sons working from home. The family attends a small, conservative, evangelical church.

The Moodys love children; they have four and are expecting twins.

Come join the Moodys for the spring!

Chapter 1

Early Morning Alarm

Eleven-year-old Max rolled over, yawned, and pulled the comforter closer. Trying to shake himself from a sleepy fog, he realized he was hearing something. *Brrriiinnnngggg, brrriiinnnngggg,* the phone rang insistently. *Who could that be?* Max tossed back his warm covers and stumbled to the door. Grasping the handle, he opened the door, and as he stepped into the hall, he no longer heard the ringing. *That's strange. Maybe I was dreaming.*

He sighed, slipped back into the bedroom, and a wet nose brushed against his hand. "Maple," he knelt down, and scratched the golden retriever's ears. "Good girl. Did you hear the phone ring, too?"

Max crawled into bed feeling very wide awake. His mind drifted to Grandma and her recent heart attack. He was glad she was out of the hospital, at home, and doing well. *The best thing is that she accepted Jesus. She is a*—Max's thoughts were interrupted by the ringing of the phone. *I guess I wasn't dreaming before!* He softly rolled from bed and hurried to the door, but this time his noise hadn't escaped his brother, Mitch. Nine-year-old Mitch's voice sounded muffled from the top bunk. "What's going on, Max?"

"I don't know; the phone's been ringing. I'll be back in a minute!" Max hoarsely whispered.

Brrriiinnnngggg, brrri—. Max heard Dad's voice from the bedroom. "Hello? Yes, we spoke a minute ago. Don't worry; I'm heading there."

Max sank down on the carpet, confused. A minute later, Dad and Mom's door opened, and Max asked, "Dad, what's happening?"

Dad, not expecting someone outside his door, jumped in surprise and then said, "The alarm at the bank went off. I need to meet the police there. You may come with me if you want; you'll need to hurry and get dressed."

"You mean the burglar alarm?"

"The security alarm."

They heard a thud and the sound of footsteps, then saw Mitch's head pop out the bedroom door. "Dad, may I come?"

"Yes, but like I told Max, you need to hurry. I'll go to the car, and you boys can meet me there."

Mom followed Dad down the stairs. She turned on the kitchen light and reached for Dad's keys. "Here you go," she handed them to Dad. "The boys will love the adventure; I hope nothing's seriously wrong."

Dad gave her a hug. "Everything should be fine; I've heard plenty of stories about how sensitive the alarms are. Our bank has never had an emergency. Try to get back to sleep for those twins."

Mom's eyes twinkled. "I will." Dad pulled on a coat and walked into the cold, dark garage.

Mom glanced at the clock and yawned. *It's only one,* she thought. Soon both boys rushed by her. "Love you," she softly called.

Dad noted the trembling boys' excitement as they tumbled into the car. Mitch was the first to burst out: "What do you think we'll find?"

Dad flicked on his headlights and backed from the driveway before he answered. "It's probably just an alarm malfunction. I really don't think it's anything, but you never know."

"What were all those phone calls about? I thought I was dreaming at first," Max rubbed his eyes in an effort to fully wake up.

Dad chuckled. "A phone call in the middle of the night definitely gets a person's attention. The first phone call was from the police. They said the alarm had gone off, they had checked the outside of the building, and everything seemed okay. They asked if I wanted to come down and have them look around inside, and I told them that I would need to."

"Why did they call you? Why not call somebody else?" Mitch wondered.

"Anthony Johnson, the man who gave us the dresser last December, is the usual contact for the alarm. He's out of town this week, and I was assigned to be the contact. I wasn't expecting anything to happen, though.

"The second call was from a man who works at the bank and lives only a block from it," Dad continued. "He could hear the alarm and wanted to let me know. I told him I was heading down there. By the way, boys, I wouldn't have brought you if I had thought there was going to be danger.

It's likely the alarm malfunctioned, but the bank wants us to go through the building each time the alarm goes off."

Dad, Max, and Mitch were quiet for the remainder of the drive. As Dad turned the corner, bright blue and red lights flashed across the bank building. Two police cars were parked facing each other, and three officers stood in front of the door. Mitch quickly recognized Officer Ruggles, the man who had been at their neighbor Mr. Delome's house after the fire several months before.

Dad pulled into a spot on the opposite side of the street and instructed, "Stay close to me, boys."

"Yes, sir," was the response. Both boys looked carefully before they crossed the street, even though everything was deserted. The sound of the alarm sirens made it impossible to talk further. Dad quickly showed the officers his bank badge and then went to the large, heavy front door and unlocked it. Dad felt along a wall, flipped on several lights,

Two police cars were parked facing each other . . .

and disarmed the alarm. He turned to the officers. "I've never done this before, but I understand that you'll do a search of the building."

"Yes, sir. We've already checked the outside, and there doesn't appear to have been a forced entry. Per your request, we'll do a search inside. Are you ready?" Officer Ruggles asked Dad.

"We are." Dad and the boys followed two of the officers as they began their search, while the third walked behind the boys.

Mitch whispered to Max, "Will we find a bank robber carrying money in a bag?"

Max realized his legs were slightly trembling, but he tried to sound brave. "The officer didn't seem to think anything was wrong. I guess we'll see."

At the sound of a loud noise, Mitch jumped and grabbed for Max. "What was THAT?" he shouted.

A young officer, who was the last of the search party, seemed amused. "It was just a door," he reassured Mitch in the dim light.

"It wasn't the bank robber?" Immediately, Mitch realized what a silly question he'd asked. *I need to learn to think about what I'm going to say before I speak,* he thought.

"No, young man. He wouldn't be that noisy. The office door got away from me."

Mitch quickened his stride, realizing that he was falling behind Dad. When the officers had searched the main part of the building, Officer Ruggles said, "We need to go downstairs."

Max's eyes widened. *The dark basement where all the boxes were stored?* He had gone down there once with Dad to find something, and it was not on his list of "want to do again" activities. Mitch whispered quietly to Max, "Does the officer mean the basement?"

Max nodded. No more words were needed between the boys. The officers walked down first, with Dad and the boys following. Shuffling around a row of boxes, one of the officers complained, "Sure is musty. You'd think a bank could afford to make their basement a little nicer. They could also improve with better lighting; it'd make a search five times easier."

"Maybe that's why we never find anyone," Office Ruggles remarked.

Max and Mitch felt relief after the officers declared the search complete. When they reached the top of the stairs, Officer Ruggles turned to Dad. "While we were waiting for you, the dispatcher said this is the second time the alarm has gone off this year. The first two incidents are free, but after that, each time is $250. You might want to look into what's making the alarm go off and see if it can be made a bit less sensitive," Officer Ruggles suggested. "I know electronic devices are difficult sometimes."

"Thanks. I won't reset it, and I'll call the technician out in the morning to look at it," Dad replied. He closed the door and locked it. The boys waited for Dad. They crossed the street together and climbed into the car. Dad asked, "How was that for a night's excitement?"

"I'd say it was incredible," Max exclaimed. "What time is it?"

Dad glanced at his watch. "Two ten."

"Dad, I must confess," Mitch said. "I was only a little scared when we were walking through the building, but I really was afraid as we started into the basement. Right at that moment, I remembered a verse I memorized last year. It goes like this: 'Fear thou not; for I *am* with thee: be not dismayed; for I *am* thy God: I will strengthen thee; yea, I will help thee; yea, I will uphold thee with the right hand of my righteousness.' I wasn't scared after that."

Dad turned his blinker on as they approached their street. "See, Son, how memorizing your Bible is wonderful! Then, at the moment of need, Jesus brought it back to your mind. Memorization is a great use of time." Before long, they were home, and Dad encouraged the boys to go right to bed.

Hours later, Max awoke with a start. The sun was shining in through the edges of his blind, and the clock read 8:34! "Mitch," he gently pulled on a sheet that was hanging from the top bunk. "Can you believe it's after 8:30?"

Mitch yawned. "I've been awake for exactly two minutes. I want to tell the girls about our adventure."

"We're going to be late for our school morning. Let's ask Mom what the plan is and then come back and have our devotions," Max suggested.

Hurrying out, the boys were surprised to see Dad in the kitchen. "There they are! I'm home from work today. I called my boss to alert him about the bank issue we had and that the alarm was not set. He told me I could enjoy a family day at home for the trouble of having to go out in the middle of the night."

"Wow!" Max grinned.

"I'm happy to be home. Mom and I've been discussing the day's plans. Mollie and Maddie did your chores. You may get dressed, have your time with Jesus, and then eat your breakfast. You should have time to complete all your main school subjects this morning. Then, in the afternoon, we'll have a practical, hands-on, learning project while Mom and the girls visit Grandma."

"Excellent. But what is the project?" Mitch wondered.

"We need to fix the leaky faucet in the back bathroom. Mom has been good not to complain about it, but I rediscovered it this morning helping Mom with laundry."

Chapter
2

Plumbing 101

After lunch, Mom and the girls left for Grandpa and Grandma's. Max and Mitch followed Dad to the small bathroom beside the laundry room. "Okay, boys, we're going to have a little plumbing lesson. We need to shut the water off underneath the sink first."

"Mitch, I'll let you do this." Dad crawled under the sink and showed Mitch where he would be turning off the water. When Mitch was in place and had begun his task, Dad knelt down watching him. "Turn it clockwise; that's right. Since the shut-off valves aren't used very often, they can be difficult to turn."

Mitch strained: "This is hard, Dad."

"Yes, Son, but keep trying."

Within a minute, Mitch announced, "Got it!" He emerged grinning.

"I knew you could do it." Dad tousled Mitch's hair. "Next step is to use the screwdriver to remove the faucet's plastic handle. Max, you can do this; first pop the plastic cover off and loosen the screw. Once the screw is out, you might have to lightly tap on the handle with the end of the screwdriver to get it off. Frequently water sediment will build up inside the handle, making it stick to the valve stem."

Max followed Dad's instructions. "Now," Dad said as he handed Max a wrench, "use this to turn the valve. We'll take the bad valve to the store so we can locate the right replacement."

On the way to the store, Dad and the boys discussed what they would need. "Max and Mitch, this would be a good opportunity for you to learn to ask questions and be able to find the part without me giving my input."

"Yes, sir," Max agreed, and Mitch nodded.

They arrived at their favorite home-improvement store and hurried to the plumbing section. An elderly man, clad in a carpenter's apron, greeted them. "Hello. May I help you?"

Max noticed his badge read, "Jake Walter," and then underneath, "10 years of service."

"Yes, sir, I hope you can. It seems you've worked at this store a long time, haven't you, Mr. Walter?" Max asked.

Mr. Walter gave a friendly squeeze to Max's shoulder. "Yes, Sonny, and most of it's been in the plumbing area; I like my work. Before this job, I was a plumber. When I retired, I decided to work here part-time; it helps occupy me."

Max showed Mr. Walter the valve, and asked him if they carried a replacement part. Mr. Walter took the valve in his hands and examined it. "Yes, sir. We have what you need." The boys and Dad followed him down the aisle. Mr. Walter placed the new valve in Max's hands. "Anything else?"

Dad laughed. "Not at the moment. You know how these plumbing projects work, though. It usually takes twice as long as you expect and three trips to the store, so we may be seeing you again."

"You're right. If you have any questions, call me. Just dial the store and ask for Jake." Mr. Walter grasped Dad's hand in a hearty shake.

Dad and the boys headed to the checkout area. "Wow, Dad!" Mitch exclaimed in amazement. "They have those self-checkouts. May we please try using one?"

"Sure."

Mitch hurried over to a small checkout station. He turned to Max and paused only momentarily and then asked in a quiet voice, "Would you like to do this?"

"I'll watch." Max could tell Mitch was eager to try out the new system.

Mitch followed the on-screen instructions. He placed the item in the bag and mourned, "Too bad we don't have a cartful. Maybe Grandpa will build a new house and buy lots of materials."

Dad inserted cash into the machine. "I don't think Grandpa has any plans for a new house."

On the way home, Max shared an idea with Dad. "We children would like to do a twin baby shower for Mom to bless her because she's the very best mom ever. I know we don't have much time left, since the twins are due in a few weeks, but would you mind if we had a baby shower next Friday? We would also invite Grandpa and Grandma."

"That's wonderful," Dad was pleased. "What are your plans?"

"Mollie and Grandma can make a cake. We're going to have a little program: Mollie, Mitch, and I will share. What else?"

"Maddie," Mitch hinted.

"That's right," Max continued. "Maddie will sing a song. We haven't finalized the rest of the details since we wanted to talk to you first."

"You have my full approval."

A few minutes later, they were home. The phone rang, and Dad answered it while the boys fixed three cups of hot chocolate and heard Dad's half of the conversation: "Hi, Matt . . . We're doing well . . . Emily is getting close with the twins; she has a few weeks left. We guys were fixing a leaky faucet, and we just came back from picking up a part. How is your family? . . . Great. Is your youngest son feeling better? . . . We've been blessed not to have the flu this year, and I'm especially grateful because of Emily and her pregnancy . . . Yes, I do remember seeing that in the newsletter recently . . . You're kind to offer, but our children don't play sports . . . To be perfectly honest, my boys get all the teamwork they need right here. Even today we're working on that plumbing project . . . Thank you for understanding. You take care, and God bless. Bye!"

Dad turned to the puzzled boys. "That was Mr. Matt Brown. He and his wife are the leaders of the homeschool group. After some chit chat, he wanted to know if you boys would like to participate on the basketball team they're starting up. Mom and I have strong feelings about why we don't want you children playing team sports. Max, do you remember playing baseball when you were eight?"

"That's right, I did! I had almost forgotten."

"Do you remember why we stopped?" Dad asked.

"Yes," Max paused. "It was for several reasons: I was picking up bad attitudes from the other boys. I also started looking to my coach as my hero instead of you. I began fussing with Mitch more and didn't want to be around him. I can't think of what else."

"You remembered well. Another reason was it was taking a lot of our time. In fact, we were having trouble finding time for our family devotions. We realized that you could learn all the things that people say are benefits of team sports right here at home."

Max and Mitch sipped their hot chocolate while they listened to Dad. "We made you a cup, Dad," Mitch said as he offered the mug.

"Thank you; I appreciate it! Let's drink this up and go to work." The phone rang again. "Maybe not quite yet," Dad added and picked up the phone. "Hello? . . . Yes, we came in several minutes ago, and Matt Brown called . . . Not quite. He wanted to know if the boys could play basketball this year . . . Matt graciously accepted the answer. How's your time going? . . . Good . . . Are you feeling okay? . . . Maddie can nap there . . . I've been forgetting to move Maddie's bed into our room for the twins. The side railings are in the basement, and the bed Grandpa gave us is propped up in the garage. The boys and I'll take a bit of time to do that when we're through with this project . . . Right . . . After we finish, we'll come on over . . . Love you, too."

Dad hung the phone up. "You could guess who that was: Mom. She and the girls are going to stay the rest of the afternoon at Grandma's. We need to move Maddie's bed into our room and put the side railings on to make it back into the baby crib. It'll be nice to get Maddie in a regular bed. I hadn't realized she was in the sideless crib for the last couple of years! The Lord provided Maddie's bed through Grandpa and Grandma. As soon as we're done with both projects, we'll go to Grandpa and Grandma's because Grandma has invited us for dinner. Maybe we can bless Grandpa before dinner by helping him with something."

Dad and the boys went back to the bathroom, and Dad took the valve out of the bag. "We're ready to finish. Max, you can put this back in—oh, there's the doorbell. I'll go get it; Maple heard it too. You boys can wait a minute."

Max and Mitch chatted until Dad reappeared with a guest. Mr. Delome grinned. "I was getting lonely at home, and I thought the Moodys might have something going on. How did I know?"

"As I was telling you," Dad stepped around Mr. Delome and stood in front of the sink. "We're finishing a plumbing project. So Max, after you put the valve in, you'll tighten it up, screw the handle back on, and we'll see if it works. Be really careful not to drop the screw into the sink drain; I've done that before."

It took Max a few minutes of working before he announced success. Max turned the water on, while Mitch checked for leaks underneath. "Oh, Dad!" Mitch's voice rang out. "One of the shut-off valves is leaking where it connects to the pipe."

"That shouldn't be hard to fix." Dad gave Mitch a wrench. "Just tighten it to the right."

Mitch accepted the offered tool and crawled back under the sink. Following a few seconds of silence, Mitch loudly proclaimed, "I'm tightening it now, Dad." Suddenly, water began shooting out from under the sink, and Mitch scrambled out, spurting and gasping. "What happened?" he shouted.

With water spraying from under the sink, Mr. Delome leaped back out of the doorway, while Dad ran to the basement to shut off the water to the house. Max and Mitch tumbled from the bathroom in an attempt to avoid the water. Mitch wiped his eyes in disbelief. "How'd I do that?"

The water flow stopped, and Dad came up from the basement with a smile. Mr. Delome shook his head. "That was close—I almost got wet, but you boys are definitely wet."

Dad laughed. "Nothing like a little plumbing excitement! I'd say you turned the wrench the wrong direction, Mitchell." He hugged Mitch.

Mitch accepted the offered tool and crawled back under the sink.

"I'm VERY sorry, Dad," Mitch apologized.

"I'm not bothered a bit; that's the way you learn lessons. I'm sure Mr. Delome has a few stories about plumbing."

"You are right!" Mr. Delome exclaimed. "Why that reminds me of the time . . ."

Chapter 3 | Midwife Visit, Shower, and Peaches

Saturday arrived, and Grandpa and Dad had their weekly Bible study. As they finished up, Dad shared with Grandpa, "I've been praying about our study, and I know the reason we started was because you wanted help in learning how to study the Bible. I feel like we've accomplished that goal, and I think it would be wonderful if you and Grandma begin studying together. It'll deepen your relationship."

Grandpa nodded. "I find it interesting you mention that because I was wondering the same thing."

Grandpa left as the children were getting up. After breakfast and morning chores, the children had a half hour free before it was time to go to the midwife appointment. Mollie came into the boys' bedroom, and Maddie trailed behind. "Let's work on the twins' shower plans," Mollie suggested.

"Good idea." Max pulled a small notebook from under his bed.

A little while later, Dad called, "Ten minutes until we leave."

When the family was settled in the van, Mollie looked at the empty seat. "Dad, what are we going to do when the twins come? We won't have room!"

"Mom and I've been praying about that, and I'd like for the whole family to be lifting this before Jesus. We have a savings account for a van, but there's not enough in it to purchase a used twelve-passenger van that is in great repair and doesn't have too many miles. Mollie, here's a question: did Jesus give us these twins?"

"Yes, sir!"

"Then He'll provide what we need. It may not be what we want, but He'll meet our needs. I figure we can get by with taking two vehicles for a while if we don't have a van large enough."

"You're right, Dad." Several minutes later, as Dad pulled in a driveway, Mollie remarked, "It was very kind of Mr. and Mrs. Gibson to invite us to visit with them while Mom has her appointment."

Miss Carolyn, who was in her early thirties and not married, lived with her parents in a mid-sized home that looked like it belonged in a small mountain town in Colorado. The outside walls were fashioned of strong logs, and pine trees surrounded the house.

As Dad helped Mom out, he commented, "It's nice that the snow has finally melted. Spring should be right around the corner!"

"I see a robin, Daddy." Maddie was delighted as she pointed to a low branch on a tree.

"You're right," Dad agreed. The family climbed a small set of stone stairs to a large, wooden front porch.

A lady with dark brown hair, sprinkled with silver, opened the front door. "Come in; Carolyn's expecting you. She'll be down in a minute; she just received a phone call." The lady bustled around taking the Moodys' coats. "It's been a long time since I've seen you children. You must have been the last little one." She smiled warmly at Maddie.

"Hi, Mrs. Gibson, I'm Maddie." Maddie introduced herself.

Mrs. Gibson's smile grew larger. Mr. Gibson, a man with light gray hair and a cheerful face, shook everyone's hands. "Aren't we glad the weather is warming up? I thought winter would never end!" He noticed the look on Mitch's face and laughed. "When you get older you'll understand."

Miss Carolyn hurried in. "Good morning! I've been looking forward to your visit." Dad and Mom followed Miss Carolyn to a nearby room.

Mr. Gibson's broad smile made the children feel at home, and he motioned to the couch and several chairs. "Please sit wherever you'd like. Mrs. Gibson and I love talking with children. Now tell me about yourselves: names, how old, what grade you're in, what you like to do, those sorts of things."

The children answered everything, but then they worked at asking their own questions. Dad and Mom had taught them that an important key to conversations was asking questions; this also demonstrated your interest in the person. Mitch was able to start with a question that he was curious about. "Mr. Gibson, are you related to the animal catcher?"

"As a matter of fact, yes; he's my younger brother. We're very different, which you've probably noticed." Mr. Gibson paused and then went on. "My biggest sorrow is that he's not saved. I've tried to share Jesus with him, but he isn't interested. Maybe someday I'll have the joy of calling him my brother in Christ."

"How long have you known Jesus Christ as your Savior?" Mollie wondered.

Mr. Gibson suddenly smiled. "There's a subject, my girl, that is hard for me to stop talking about. Right after Mrs. Gibson and I were married, we started going to church. I really wasn't interested, but Mrs. Gibson thought that was the thing to do, so being a dutiful husband, I decided to go along with her. It was about two months later that I was convicted of my sin and went down to the front of the church crying out to Jesus to save me. I was twenty-five years old. Mrs. Gibson was a bit shocked—but she noticed such a difference in my life that she couldn't complain. The following Sunday, she accepted Jesus as her Lord and Savior."

"I like that salvation story," Mitch nodded.

"Do any of you play instruments?" Mrs. Gibson asked.

"Only the piano," Max said. "What about you?"

"Not really, but Miss Carolyn can play the piano well, although she's been too busy lately for that. Piano is a fine instrument to give you a good musical foundation, especially if you're interested in other instruments."

Mom's appointment passed too swiftly for the children, and it was time to leave. They thanked Mr. and Mrs. Gibson several times. "Well, I wish we could have you back again, but I think your mom will be having the twins before much longer! Maybe we'll see you with your mom's next baby," Mrs. Gibson laughed.

After Mr. Gibson distributed the Moodys' coats, he walked them out. Mr. Gibson laid his hand on Dad's shoulder and spoke quietly. "Your children were a joy. I know it's because of the Lord Jesus Christ."

"Thank you. Have a blessed day!"

That afternoon, Mom and Maddie took naps, and the rest stayed in the living room. Dad worked through the family's finances, and the other three read. Max was interested in learning computer programming, so Dad had bought a book for him to study. Mitch was working through a plumbing book, and Mollie was reading a beginner's sewing book Grandma had loaned her. The doorbell rang, followed by an instantaneous pounding on the front door. A bit startled, Dad jumped up. "Who could that be?" He quickly opened the door.

Mr. Russell wordlessly half-threw his cat, Peaches, and a bag into Dad's arms. He turned and sprinted down the steps, shouting over his shoulder, "My wife's in labor; I'll call you later."

Dad stepped out and watched as Mr. Russell backed from the driveway and sped away. Max joined him. "I guess he was in a big hurry."

"You're right." Dad handed the cat to Max and turned to go inside. Maple, who had awakened from her nap because of the activity, squeezed through the half-open door and looked at the new visitor.

Peaches' hair bristled, and she meowed loudly. Max felt her claws dig into his shirt. "Peaches, it's just Maple!" He tried to grasp Peaches tightly, but it was too late. With a flash of orange and yellow fur, Peaches leapt from Max's arms and raced across the front yard. Maple followed in hot pursuit.

Max chased the two animals, with Mollie and Mitch, who had heard the commotion, following close behind. Peaches climbed into their neighbor's tree, and Maple barked at the base of the tree frantically scraping her paws on the bark, as if trying to climb the tree herself. "Now what are we going to do?" Mollie sighed.

Peaches meowed unhappily perched in the crook of the tree. "It would not be good to lose her while the Russells are gone," Mitch said. "I was surprised at how fast an older cat could run; I guess she had great motivation!" He glanced back at the house. "Oh, there's Dad."

"Maple!" Dad called loudly. "Come here." Maple turned at the sound of the voice and hesitated for a moment before obeying Dad.

"I guess we'll need the step ladder. At least she didn't climb the really tall tree," Max observed.

Mollie and Mitch watched Peaches for several minutes while Max went to find the ladder. Peaches did not budge from the safe haven in the tree. Max soon returned with the

. . . Maple barked at the base of the tree frantically scraping her paws on the bark, as if trying to climb the tree herself.

ladder. "Would you please stand here at the base and make sure it stays steady for me?" Max requested.

"Okay." Mollie and Mitch each held a side.

"Here, Peaches." Max reached tentatively for the cat, who still seemed upset. "I wonder if Peaches bites," Max mused. Surprising him, Peaches crawled toward Max, pitifully meowing. Max reached out and firmly took her in his arms. "Got her!" He carefully held the cat in one arm while stepping down the ladder.

"I'll put the ladder away," Mitch offered. The children walked across the yard to their house.

Inside, Dad was still working on finances. "Good job, children. I thought it might be a while before you could coax her down. Why don't you put Peaches in the back room, Max? It'll be best to keep some distance between Maple and her."

Sunday morning dawned, and Max and Mitch struggled to awaken. "It's seven o'clock," Max announced. "We need to get up now because we have to care for Peaches."

Max felt the bunk bed move slightly as Mitch rolled over. "Okay." Mitch let out a loud yawn.

Dad poked his head in the door. "Are my boys awake? It's time to get up because you have your Bible time, breakfast, and taking care of Peaches to do before church. We have to leave a little earlier since Grandma Clifton's going to church with us." Grandma Clifton was an elderly widow who lived around the corner from the Moodys, and over the last year they had enjoyed helping her.

"Yes, sir." Max threw back his covers and grabbed his Bible from beside his bed. When the boys finished reading their Bibles and praying, they hurried to prepare for the day.

Mitch was ready first. "I'll meet you downstairs," he said. "I'll work on warming up the insulin shot for Peaches."

A few minutes later, Max joined Mitch in the back room. Peaches stood next to Mitch, pressed against his leg and purring happily. "Would you give Peaches her shot? I don't like to," Mitch confessed.

"Sure." Max gently pulled up the loose skin on Peaches' neck and administered the shot. Mitch filled her food bowl, and Max petted Peaches. "You can eat your breakfast." The boys closed the door as they left so that Maple wouldn't cause problems.

Max and Mitch found Dad in the kitchen. "How'd it go?" Dad asked, dropping an egg shell into the trash.

"Peaches didn't fuss at all about her shot, which was nice," Max responded.

"That reminds me," Dad turned to the boys. "Mr. Russell called. He said Mrs. Russell had a baby boy early this morning. She and the baby are doing well. They've named him Madison David. Mrs. Russell and Madison will be in the hospital until Tuesday. I told him we'd love to bring them a meal Thursday evening. He said that'd be great because he doesn't cook much—boxed macaroni and cheese is the limit. He asked about Peaches; I told him she was fine. Mr. Russell said that we can bring her back on Thursday, if we're okay keeping her that long."

The next day, when school was finished, Max, Mollie, and Mitch took Maple on a walk while Mom and Maddie napped. "Isn't it exciting about the twins?" Max sighed. "I can hardly believe they'll be here soon."

"It is exciting; I like to think about two brand new tiny babies in our family," Mitch mused.

Heading home, they rounded the corner near Grandma Clifton's and saw Mr. Delome starting out on a walk. He waved a gloved hand. "How is everyone on this beautiful day?"

"We're blessed, Mr. Delome."

"How is your mom feeling? Isn't she about to have the twins?" Mr. Delome asked.

Max nodded. "Yes sir; she's due in a few weeks, but the midwife thinks the babies may come early. Whenever anyone asks her how she's feeling, she says she's doubly blessed. We're trying to help a lot, and we're going to give her a surprise twin baby shower."

"Really? I've never been to a baby shower, but my wife always enjoyed them."

"We only had the idea last week, so we're planning it quickly," Mollie explained. "Between working on the shower, doing school, helping Mom, and pet-sitting Peaches, we're busy."

"You do seem to keep busy. What do you do at a baby shower?"

"Well, I've only been to one," Mollie explained. "That was for Maddie, and I don't remember much. Grandma has given us ideas, and we've decided to make ours different from the normal shower."

"I'm sure you'll come up with something excellent."

After they said good-bye, the children continued their walk. Mitch broke the silence: "I think Mr. Delome wants to come to the shower."

Max prompted, "Why not? He'd love it! Let's ask Dad tonight if we can invite him."

That evening, Max felt an unusual anticipation at bedtime, knowing that he would have the opportunity to talk to Dad about Mr. Delome. "It's still ten more minutes until Dad comes to pray with us," Max sighed. "What shall we do, Mitch?"

"Let's work on our Scripture memory. We're supposed to do a review for Dad this weekend, and my verses are a little rough."

"That's a great suggestion."

A little while later, Dad came into the boys' room to pray with them. "Dad, we were on a walk today, and we talked with Mr. Delome," Max started. "We told him about the twins' baby shower, and he seemed quite interested in it. Would it be okay if we invited him?"

"Max, that's a fine idea, and I know he'll enjoy it. In fact, why not invite Grandma Clifton and Mrs. Bagwell?"

The next morning, Mollie was quietly reading her Bible when Maddie bounced out of bed. "Mollie, have the twins comed yet?"

"Not yet. We have to wait longer. But, we're glad they haven't been born yet, because we're going to do that secret for Mom, remember?"

"I remember. I do hope they come soon 'cause I like babies."

After breakfast, Max called Mr. Delome, who immediately accepted the invitation. "Gifts? Well, yes, if you care to . . .

Mom doesn't have a list made up, so whatever you want . . . We're just happy you can come . . ."

That afternoon, the children asked Mom how they could help her. "You are such a blessing," Mom smiled. "The first thing that comes to mind is that area outside the front of the house; it's been bothering me. There are leaves around the bushes and also dead weeds from last summer. Since the snow has melted, it shouldn't be hard to get cleaned up. Today's pretty nice; I guess it's fifty-two now," Mom finished, glancing at the thermometer.

"No problem!" Max assured Mom. "Are you going to take a nap?"

She shook her head. "I'm not tired, but I have some correspondence to catch up on, so I'll be in my bedroom if you need anything. I love you all!"

The children gathered the needed supplies and went to the front yard. "There's lots of leaves," Mollie commented. Discussing the upcoming shower helped time pass for the children.

Suddenly, Mollie heard a voice which sounded like Mrs. Maud Bagwell, an elderly friend of the Moodys who lived several houses up the street. "Hello, Oliver," Mrs. Bagwell called, as she neared the Moodys' driveway. Mollie poked her head around the bush. She saw Mrs. Bagwell wave at Mr. Delome, who was getting his mail.

Mollie was debating about saying "hi" but since it was obvious Mrs. Bagwell didn't see her, she was quiet. "Maud, I want to talk to you," Mr. Delome motioned with his mail.

With quick, firm steps, Mrs. Bagwell crossed over to his side of the street. "What's on your mind, Oliver?"

"I've been invited to the Moodys' twin baby shower!"

"The WHAT?"

"The twin baby shower!"

Without realizing it, Max, Mollie, and Mitch stopped working as they listened to the loud conversation. "Oliver Delome, you're not telling me the whole story. Why I was talking to Emily Moody the other day, and she didn't mention anything."

"That's because it's a surprise," Mr. Delome said importantly. "I've always wanted to go to a baby shower. By the way, what do you have in your pocket?"

Max grinned at Mitch because they both knew what Mrs. Bagwell carried. "Why, Snickers," Mrs. Bagwell said as she reached in her pocket.

"My favorite candy bar," Mr. Delome teased.

"Oliver, you know it's my pet rat. Are you going to the twin baby shower? I wish I could come!"

"I'm going," Mr. Delome nodded. "But I don't know who they invited except for their own family, and maybe they haven't finished inviting everybody. I'll be seeing you around, Maud. Have a splendid day!"

Max went back to pulling out leaves from the bush. "I should've called and invited Mrs. Bagwell this morning. I'll do that when we get inside."

Chapter 4

Preparing for the Big Event

The next two days went quickly as Max, Mollie, and Mitch focused on school, helping Mom, and preparing for the shower. Dad had taken the children shopping for the twins' shower gifts Wednesday evening. It was now Thursday, March 3rd, the day before the big event.

Mid-afternoon when school was finished, Max, Mollie, and Mitch worked on fixing the Russells' meal. Max read aloud the list Mom had written. "Potato soup, corn, whole wheat rolls, and brownies. Those should be wonderful!"

Mom sat in a dining room chair, which Mitch had carried into the kitchen for her. "Although I think I have enough energy to prepare the whole meal, Dad encouraged me to simply watch. He says I need to be getting plenty of rest for the twins' birth."

Walking into the room at that moment, Mollie caught the last part of Mom's sentence and glanced at Mom. *I hope the twins don't come before the shower,* she thought. After the soup was simmering on the stove and the roll dough was rising, Mom smiled. "I'm hungry for a good orange."

"You're still having cravings?" Mitch asked.

"Yes. The sad part is I finished our final orange at midnight. The twins were pretty active, so I got up to read my Bible. Then, an orange sounded good, and I was glad to find we had one left. I'm going to sew for an hour, but first I'll call Dad and see if he can buy a bag of oranges on the way home from work. I love each of you!" With that, Mom went upstairs.

Max peeled a potato as he commented, "I know Dad's going to the store because he said he'd buy the food items we need for the shower. Then he'll drop by Grandpa and Grandma's to leave our things there for tomorrow's baking."

Maddie came down from her nap at four o'clock and wanted to help. Max was mixing up the brownies while Mollie plopped the roll dough onto the counter. "You may help me," Max offered. "Here, you can stand on this chair."

Maddie bobbed her blonde, curly ponytail as she climbed onto the chair. "I like to help you."

Mollie pinched off sections of dough and shaped them into balls, which she set on greased cookie sheets.

Mitch lifted the lid on the pot. "This smells yummy; I hope there's some left for us. I'm going to check on Peaches." The week of pet-sitting had been pretty uneventful as long as Peaches stayed in the back room away from Maple.

Mollie pinched off sections of dough and shaped them into balls, which she set on greased cookie sheets. Maddie happily worked with Max on the brownies. At five thirty, dinner was ready to be taken to the Russells. The phone rang, and it was Grandma for Mom. Dad handed over the phone. "You go ahead and talk to Grandma; we'll take the meal to the Russells."

"Thank you, Jim. Please tell Kim 'hi' for me. I'm anxious to get to visit with her soon and see Madison."

Dad helped the children load the van with the meal while Max carried Peaches out. They drove up the street, and Dad parked in the driveway. "I'll carry the soup pot; Mitch, you may grab the bag of rolls and container of corn; Mollie, please get the pan of brownies. Max, I guess that leaves you with handling Peaches."

"Daddy," Maddie tugged on his shirt sleeve, "I can wing the doibell."

"Sure. Remember what Mom's been working with you on? Rrrrrring the doorrrrrrrrrbell."

"Yes, sirrrrrr. May I rrrring the doorrrbell?"

"Yes, you may. You did that very well!"

Maddie had barely completed her task when Mr. Russell popped the door open. Mitch wondered if he was hungry and had been waiting for his food. Mr. Russell smiled. "Thank you for bringing us dinner and Peaches. Step right on in." They walked into the warm, cozy house.

Mrs. Russell was sitting in the living room. "It's the Moodys! Welcome!"

"Hello," Dad and the children greeted her.

Mrs. Russell continued: "Thanks for taking care of Peaches. It was silly, but I was so concerned about leaving her when we needed to go to the hospital. I knew we could have a neighbor come over, but I didn't feel good leaving her here alone. In fact, as Dave can affirm, I was getting upset. He suggested the life-saving idea of bringing her over to y'all's house. I've missed her, but I admit, Madison has consumed all of my time. Plus Peaches isn't the 'baby' anymore, if you know what I mean." She took Peaches from Max. "She's looking amazingly healthy for a medically challenged cat!"

Mr. Russell sniffed the air. "Whatever you brought smells wonderful!" he remarked as he eyed the food the Moodys were placing on the counter. "How'd pet-sitting go? Did Maple like Peaches?"

Mitch quickly replied, "No. When you left, Peaches jumped out of Max's arms, and we had a little dog-cat chase. Peaches ended up in our neighbors' tree."

Mrs. Russell giggled. "That's not surprising. I hadn't even considered Maple and Peaches not doing well together."

"It worked out fine," Dad reassured Mrs. Russell. "Peaches stayed in the back room away from Maple, and the children spent time with her."

"We're grateful to you for taking care of Peaches." Mr. Russell pulled out a twenty-dollar bill. "Please take it," he said as Max was shaking his head. "If you want us to call you again; this is important. I can't tell you how relieved Kim was to know you were taking care of her cat."

Max took the offered money. "Thank you, sir."

"Would you like to see Madison? He's sleeping at the moment, but I peek at him all the time. It doesn't bother him." Mrs. Russell led them back to a bedroom and turned on a lamp.

Maddie sucked in her breath. "I like the baby! Will the twins be like that?"

Dad nodded and whispered back, "Yes, they will." They came out of the room, and Mrs. Russell asked Dad about Mom. "Emily's doing very well; you would hardly know by the way she's feeling that she's expecting twins. She isn't with us now because my mom called as we were leaving to bring the meal over. Emily's wanting to stop by sometime to talk to you and see Madison."

"I'd enjoy that."

Mr. Russell sighed. "I admire your family. We're trying to get used to this parenting thing. One baby has been hard enough. I can't imagine y'all going from four children to six!"

Dad chuckled. "I think, though, there is a major adjustment with the first baby, since it's been just the two of you. As you continue having more children, you'll find you have your own little built-in helpers who will be happy to be a blessing. The children have been a major help with Emily expecting twins."

When they came home from the Russells, Mom was in the living room, reading her Bible. She closed it and asked about their visit. Max filled her in and then inquired about what Mom had done while they were gone. "I've only been reading my Bible for a minute or two. Grandma had a surprising idea. She wondered if she and Grandpa could take care of you children tomorrow. She said that would give me time by myself to rest or get things done for the twins. She even offered to help you children with school. I have thought about trying to get some things done before the twins are born—like filing papers, putting pictures into albums, projects like that—but I didn't want to take off school knowing we would be having a break after the twins are born. You can get your seat work done in the morning and then have some free time with Grandpa and Grandma in the afternoon."

"I like that idea," Dad was pleased. "We don't know how much longer until the twins come. I'll take the children to Grandpa and Grandma's on my way to work."

After dinner and family devotions, the children met in the girls' room to discuss preparations for the twins' baby shower. "Maddie needs help with her song," Mollie said.

"Okay, and I should work on my speech," Max agreed. "Mitch, could you sing a few songs in our bedroom to cover up the noise Maddie'll be making?"

Mitch looked sheepish. "I'll feel silly, but I'll do it!"

The boys slipped into their room, and Mollie waited for Mitch to begin. A minute went by and then another, until a loud voice rang out: "When the trumpet of the Lord shall sound. . . ."

"Okay, Maddie. Let's sing your song."

Mitch's fast rendition of the song continued: "When the roll, is called up yonder!"

Maddie almost shouted into Mollie's ear, "I can't remember because Mitch is singing!"

A knock was heard, and Mollie froze but then realized the knock hadn't been on her door. Mom called, "Mitch, could you quiet down a little bit?"

"Yes, ma'am!"

Maddie shrugged her shoulders. "If I can't remembers it, I can't."

"Just try. I'll help you start. I think you can go on by yourself."

Finally, Maddie had practiced her song, and Max's speech was finished. The children felt the next morning could not come soon enough!

That night Max was restless; he glanced at the clock every hour. Finally, he knew it must be time to get up, but he was disappointed to see it was only five. *I wish I was this wide awake every morning,* he thought. Max decided to pray, and soon, he was dozing off. Then Dad's voice was heard: "Good morning." Dad opened the girls' bedroom door and then the boys'. "This *is* the day *which* the LORD hath made; we will rejoice and be glad in it."

The children hurried to get ready for their exciting day. Maddie's first words were, "Have the twins comed yet?"

Mom, who was going downstairs to fix breakfast, stopped as she heard the question. "No, Sweetie. See?" Mom stood in the doorway, and it was obvious she was still expecting the twins. "In fact, would you like to feel them? They are moving a lot."

Mom sat on the bed and took one of Maddie's hands, placing it on her stomach. Maddie held perfectly still, as she intently waited. Her face lit up. "I felt it, Mommy! They did kick!"

Mollie brushed her hair and stood next to Mom. "May I feel too, Mom?"

"Yes. Try over here." It wasn't long before Mollie felt a strong kick. "I can't wait until we can hold them. Do you need help with breakfast, Mom?"

"No. I'm doing a quick, easy one since you children are going with Dad."

At breakfast, Max asked, "What are you going to do with your free time?"

"I've already made a list," Mom responded. "There's sewing to finish—I've been working on matching jumpers for us girls. I also want to organize in my room. Don't worry; I won't move around anything heavy."

Maddie reached for the jar of peanut butter and in the process knocked over her glass of milk. Maple eagerly began lapping up the drips that were coming from the table. Maddie apologized. "I'm terribly sorry. I shouldn't have bereached for the peanut butter."

Mitch, who had wisely evaded the spilled milk by a quick exit from his seat, raced from the table to grab a few rags. He mopped up the milk, and Mollie poured Maddie a new glass. "Five minutes until we leave," Dad reminded, looking at the clock. The children managed to contain their excitement while preparing to leave. They each gave Mom a hug and hurried to the van.

Chapter 5

Grandpa and Grandma's House

Dad pulled into Grandpa and Grandma's large circle driveway. Grandpa stepped out of the door and strode over to the van. "How are my grandchildren and son today?" he boomed cheerfully.

"We're blessed. Is Grandma still feeling well?" Dad wondered.

"Better than ever!" Grandpa replied. "She's looking forward to helping with the shower. Does Emily suspect anything?"

"Not that I can tell. I'm going to call her at lunch and invite her out to dinner. I'll tell her that you and Grandma are coming over to watch the children. Emily's never had a surprise party; I don't think she has any idea."

Grandpa nodded. "I get to be a school teacher this morning; it's a trade I've never tried. We'll take the children home mid-afternoon when we're through."

Dad finished helping the girls out of the van. "You'll make a good teacher, Dad. Children, remember to be praying about the shower tonight. Mr. Delome and Mrs. Bagwell aren't saved yet."

"Yes, sir!"

The children waved to Dad and then hurried into the house, chatting happily with Grandpa. Grandma, who had been opening the curtains in the living room, came over and gave them each a hug. "Good morning! How is everyone?"

Several minutes of small talk occurred before Grandma explained the schedule. "We'll do school this morning, and then before lunch, we'll bake the cake. This afternoon, we'll decorate the cake while you boys work with Grandpa on the platform you're going to build."

"What platform?" Maddie asked.

"We want something to stand on at the baby shower when we're giving our speeches and such, so Grandpa suggested we make a wooden platform," Max explained.

"Oh."

Grandma kept Maddie occupied throughout the morning with coloring books and going through her ABC flashcards. Soon, school was completed. "Well," Grandpa stood up. "Max and Mitch, let's go down to my shop and gather our supplies. Martha, please call us for lunch."

"Sure thing." The cake mix was sitting on the counter. A measuring cup contained water and oil, and Grandma grabbed a few eggs from the refrigerator. "You may go ahead and start on the cake. Would you girls like to use my aprons?" Opening the pantry door, Grandma fingered several cute aprons.

"Yes, ma'am." Mollie and Maddie each chose one.

Mollie handed Maddie the large wooden spoon. "You may stir it for me, okay?"

Grandma worked on preparing lunch while the girls made the cake. After a few minutes, the creamy mix was smooth and ready for the pan. "It smells delicious even before it is in the oven, Grandma!" Mollie poured the rich chocolate batter into the cake pan. "Oh NO!" she wailed.

Grandma turned. "What is it?"

"I forgot to grease the pan. What should I do?"

"Is that all?" Grandma sighed with relief. "Don't worry; we'll dump it back into the bowl, wash the pan, and grease it. I've done that before."

When the mistake was fixed, Grandma slid the cake pan into the oven, and she and the girls finished making lunch. "Would you like to call the boys?" Grandma asked Maddie.

"Yes, ma'am. I like to tell people it's time to eat." Maddie bounced off to the basement.

The boys and Grandpa joined them, and Grandpa asked Max to bless the food. "Dear Heavenly Father, thank You for this food that Grandma and the girls made. Please bless it. I pray that we would be diligent in getting everything done. I pray that Mom wouldn't guess what we're doing, and we would be a blessing to her. Please keep the twins safe and healthy. I pray You would also help us to find a van so we can ride together. In Jesus' Name, Amen."

Conversation revolved around the afternoon's plans. "How are we going to make our platform?" Mitch wondered.

"I've been thinking about that." Grandpa placed a slice of tomato on his bread. "It only needs to hold the weight of each of you children, right? No adult will be standing on it."

Max nodded. "Yes, sir."

"I have several old pine boards. They're not that strong, but they should hold for what we're needing."

Grandma buttered a piece of bread. "I'm excited to do cake decorating with you girls. The cake!" She jumped up and hurried to the oven. Pulling the cake out, she poked a tooth-pick in the center. "Yes, it's done. I forgot to set the timer."

"Grandma," Maddie paused and hurriedly chewed her mouthful of food. "Do I have to take a nap?"

"Yes, your mom said you need to. You may sleep in our special guest room."

Maddie speared a piece of apple, and then she looked at Grandma. "I like naps in your guest room."

"I'm glad. First, though, you can help Mollie with the frosting."

The boys cleared the lunch items and then went downstairs with Grandpa. Grandma turned on a hymn CD. "Grandpa gave this to me recently. I would never have listened to it before I became a Christian, but I love it now. My life has changed so much since I accepted Jesus as my Lord and Savior." She hunted through her recipe box and located the frosting recipe. "Here, Maddie, you may take this over to Mollie." Grandma set out the ingredients. "We're ready to begin."

Maddie poured in each ingredient when Mollie gave her permission. The white, creamy frosting took shape as Mollie turned the mixer to a higher speed. Grandma watched her youngest granddaughter and said, "Maddie, it's important you keep your fingers away from the mixing bowl. If your fingers get in the bowl while it's beating, it could really hurt them."

"Yes, ma'am." Maddie eyed the yummy-looking substance. "May I have a lick?"

Grandma peeked into the bowl. "Soon, Maddie. We'll let it beat a little longer, and then when it's done, you're welcome to a bite. We ought to test what we make."

A minute later, Mollie turned off the mixer. "Is that enough?"

"Yes," Grandma grabbed two spoons from the silverware drawer. "Tell me what you think."

The frosting passed the girls' taste test. "Time for your nap, Maddie," Grandma announced cheerfully.

Down in the basement, Grandpa and the boys were enjoying themselves. "How big are you wanting this platform to be?" Grandpa wondered, after listening to Mitch describe the object.

Mitch looked at Max. "Go ahead, Max."

"That *is* a good question. I don't want to fall off it. I know I have a tendency to fidget and move around. But if it's too big, that'll be a bother. What are your thoughts, Grandpa?"

"The wood will probably limit us on what size we can make. Let's look through what I have." Grandpa walked over to his wood bin and found several pieces. He pulled out his tape measure and pencil and made a few grunts as he calculated. "We could make it about two feet long and a foot wide."

Grandpa marked several places on the wood so they would know where to trim off the edges, and then he let Max carefully cut the pieces. "Can we paint our platform when we're finished?" Mitch asked.

"No. The problem is we don't have enough time to let it dry," Grandpa decided.

"That's fine, Grandpa; I just wondered. Mom would not appreciate a wet-paint platform in her living room!" exclaimed Mitch.

It didn't take long for the platform to be put together with Grandpa's wood glue. Mitch was anxious: "May I test it out?"

"Not yet, Mitch," Grandpa chuckled at Mitch's enthusiasm. "We have to let the glue dry first. It's a special kind—very strong—but it still takes a few hours to set up. When I bring it over tonight, you can test it."

Upstairs in the kitchen, Grandma and Mollie were beginning to work on decorating the cake. Grandma had already removed the cake from the pan onto a covered wooden board. The cake was cool and ready to frost. Grandma showed Mollie how to place several globs of frosting on the top of the cake. "This way it's easier to work with, and you have less chance of bringing up cake crumbs into your frosting. It's important to smooth it out gently," Grandma cautioned, and she used her spatula to demonstrate. "You try it."

Mollie took the offered spatula and began to spread the icing. Grandma brought down a small box from the cupboard. "What's that, Grandma?" Mollie's gaze shifted.

"These are my cake decorating supplies; I keep my icing colors, bags for the icing, and decorating tips—" Grandma stopped abruptly.

Mollie glanced back at her project and gasped. "What've I done?" With dismay, Mollie saw several small chunks of cake clinging to the frosting-laden spatula. "How did that happen?"

Grandma felt impatience rise in her heart, but she quickly rebuked the urge to fuss at Mollie. "It's okay, Mollie. We can fix it. It's because you lifted the spatula up, instead of keeping it down and close to the frosting. It happens easily when the frosting is thick; I should've made it thinner. Don't worry, Mollie. It's really my fault."

Grandma soon had expertly patched the frosting mishap, and Mollie finished covering the cake with frosting. Finally, they were ready to work on mixing the colors of decorating icing. While Mollie picked the colors she wanted to use, Grandma scooped the frosting into several bowls. Then Grandma squeezed a few drops of food coloring into each one, letting Mollie stir them up.

By this time, the boys and Grandpa had come upstairs. "We're done with our platform, and I realized I need to run to the bank. The boys and I'll be back in about a half hour." Grandpa noticed the frosting. "Do you mind if we try some?" he couldn't resist asking.

"Not at all, James." Grandma found three spoons. "While you're gone, Mollie and I will finish decorating the cake, and I'll wake Maddie from her nap soon. What time do we plan to take the children back?"

"Probably about threeish."

Three o'clock came rapidly. The boys admired Grandma and Mollie's cake. "I would've thought that you bought the cake at the store," Mitch complimented.

"Thank you, but really, Grandma helped a lot. She's very good at cake decorating," Mollie sent the praise to Grandma.

Grandpa noticed Maddie, who was trying to put on her shoes. "Maddie girl, what do you think about having twins in your family?"

"I think they'll be cute and like my babies. Remember those dollies I have?"

"I do; they are fine babies."

Soon, the Moody children were home. Mom had written a note and left it on the living room floor.

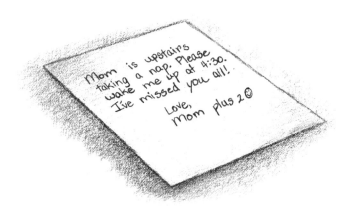

Max hung his coat in the closet. "I feel like I'm going to burst with excitement, so I'm glad Mom isn't down here yet," he finished with a whisper.

"Since we don't have much left to do for the shower until Dad and Mom leave, let's work on memory verses," Mitch suggested. "Dad gave us a new assignment yesterday."

Five minutes later, a knock was heard. *Surely this couldn't be someone for the shower? We told everyone seven o'clock.* A glance at Mollie and Mitch's faces told the same story. Maddie giggled. "It's probably for the shower."

"Shhhh . . ." Mollie instructed.

Max looked out the window. "It's the mailman!" he said, relief flooding his voice.

He opened the door. "Hello, Mr. Hunter. How are you?"

"Pretty good, although I'd be better if I were done for the day. Here's a package for the Moody twins. By the way, are they due soon?" Mr. Hunter handed a brown box and several pieces of mail to Max.

"In two and a half weeks. Often twins come early—it could be soon. Thank you, Mr. Hunter!"

When the children had finished studying their memory verses, they worked ahead on school. A few minutes before five, footsteps were heard on the stairs. Mom walked slower than usual, and Max thought there were several sleep marks on her face.

Max suddenly realized they had forgotten to wake Mom at 4:30. "Oh, Mom! I'm sorry we forgot to wake you up. Please forgive me."

"It's okay. I must have needed the extra sleep. Dad will be home anytime to take me out for dinner. How was your day with Grandpa and Grandma?" Mom seemed distracted as she went to the kitchen.

The children followed her. "Just great!" Mitch answered and then continued, "I even got through my math lesson, and Grandpa thought I did it well."

"We ate sandwiches for lunch with spicy cheese," Mollie shared. "Where are you going to eat with Dad tonight?" Mollie tried to change the subject.

"I told Dad I've been hungry for pizza!"

"Someone talking about me?" Dad called, walking in. Maple bounded for him, and he gave her a quick pat. "Are you ready?" he asked Mom. "You look beautiful."

"Do I? I feel extremely big; I was going to wear my corduroy jumper, but I discovered I don't fit into it! I wore it with Maddie when I was 9 months pregnant, but with the twins, it's a different story. Oh, Jim! I totally forgot to figure out what the children should eat tonight. Where are Grandpa and Grandma?" Mom's words came out jumbled. "I'm still not thinking clearly since waking up from my nap."

The doorbell rang, and Max ran to answer it. Grandpa and Grandma bustled in. "Sorry we're late."

Dad went to the front closet and pulled out Mom's coat. "Don't worry about the children, Dearsie. Grandma can figure out something. We'll see you later."

Before Dad closed the door to the garage, he smiled back at the children. When the garage door had shut, Grandma laughed. "Your mom has no idea what's going to happen! Grandpa ordered pizza, which should arrive in a half hour."

The children cleaned the living room until the pizza came, and then they took a break. After that, the next hour was spent with more cleaning, hanging decorations, setting up the dining room for dessert, and looking over the event schedule.

Chapter 6

The Shower

At exactly two minutes to seven, the doorbell rang. Max answered and found Grandma Clifton. "Good evening!" she greeted them.

"I'll hang up your coat," Max offered.

Grandma hugged Grandma Clifton. "It's been a long time since I've seen you. I'll be happy to take your present. How did you carry such a big gift?" Grandma wondered.

"Maybe it was my missionary experience."

The doorbell rang again; this time it was Mr. Delome. The children were surprised by his new outfit: navy pants and a striped dress shirt. His gray hair was combed neatly, and his beard was trimmed. He carried a huge package. Mitch reached out to take the package but almost dropped it. "What's in here?" Mitch exclaimed as Grandpa came to his rescue.

"Now, Mitch, do you really think I'm going to tell you?" Mr. Delome shook his head. "A present is a present."

"You're right," Mitch agreed.

Max closed the front door and took Mr. Delome's coat. Mr. Delome seemed excited. "I can't wait to see what a baby shower is like. Do you need help with anything?"

Max glanced around the room. Balloons were tied to many different items, yellow and blue streamers were hung across the fireplace, and a "Welcome Twins" banner was strung over the front window. "We should be ready."

"Hello!" A loud voice came from outside and then a knock followed.

Max opened the door and greeted Mrs. Bagwell. "Come in!"

"I was almost late because I burned my dinner. I tried to hurry as I didn't want to spoil the surprise by arriving late."

"The plan," Max started, "is for us to sit in the dark. When Dad and Mom walk in, we'll switch on the lights and shout 'Surprise!'"

Several chairs had been placed near the couch, which had a neatly-printed "Reserved for Guests of Honor" sign on it. The platform was on the edge of the circle. Everyone found a spot to sit, and Mitch took care of the lights. Soon, headlights turned into the driveway. The anticipation in the air could almost be felt. It seemed like Dad and Mom were taking an unusually long time to come in the house. Finally, they heard a door open, and Dad was talking. "Well, next time, we'll have the twins."

"Yes," Mom answered. "It sure is quiet and dark—maybe Grandpa and Grandma are doing devotions in one of the children's rooms tonight."

Mitch flipped on the lights, and everyone shouted, "SURPRISE!" as Dad and Mom rounded the corner.

Mom gasped. At that moment, Mollie decided she had never seen her mom look more beautiful. It took Mom a few seconds to collect her thoughts. No words of explanation were necessary as the room told the story. "I'm in shock! This was totally unexpected." Tears welled up and began sliding down Mom's cheeks.

"Here, Mom," Max said. "We have a special seat for you and Dad."

Max led his parents to the couch. "Here's the seat of honor." Then, Max gingerly stepped onto the platform. Mollie, Mitch, and Maddie plopped down on the carpet. "Welcome, everyone!" Max began. "We're glad you came to our baby shower for the Moody twins. The due date, or as Miss Carolyn calls it, the guess date, is not for two weeks, but the mama thinks they may arrive sooner. We're happy they waited, because this shower is important. I've asked Mr. James Moody, who is my grandpa, to open us with prayer."

Grandpa stood, making sure not to get on the homemade platform. "Let's pray. Heavenly Father, we thank You for this evening. What an incredible gift and blessing children are. We marvel at the gift of two precious babies to the Moody family. Please protect and keep them safe. May these two sweet babies accept You as their Lord and Savior when they are old enough to realize their sin and need of a Savior. In Jesus' Holy, Awesome, and Wonderful Name, Amen."

Mollie whispered to Maddie, who was eyeing the platform. Maddie seemed doubtful. "Do I stand on that thing, Max?"

"Yes. Right in the middle," Max instructed.

Maddie held a red rose and smiled, facing her parents. "Okay, Mommy, I've been wookin', I mean worrrrrkin' on a song—did I doos that rrrrright?"

Mom nodded.

In a loud but melodious voice, Maddie sang:

"My mommy is goin' to have twins,
She is the best mommy.
She loves Jesus,
And so does my daddy.
Thank You Jesus for the babies,
We'll love and caiah, I mean care, for them so well.
We just—" Maddie paused.

"I forgots the west, I mean rrrrrrest. But," she jumped off the platform and handed Mom the rose. "It's for you. The rest of my song was going to tell you about that. I love you!"

Mom's eyes overflowed with tears again, and she hugged her youngest daughter. "I love you too! You did your song so nicely."

Mitch, who hadn't been feeling nervous until now, strode to the platform. He stood on it carefully, unknowingly reaching for his pocket where his back up notes were securely stored. Or, at least they had been. With rising panic, he realized they weren't there. Clearing his throat and swallowing back the lump in it, he began: "Mom, I decided instead of a fancy speech, I'd do it this way. I will pick up my bedroom each morning; I will not leave my shoes by the back door; I will empty the twins' diaper pail—even if it's a big one; I will help you with their laundry; I will hold them when they cry; I will not complain about my schoolwork; I will love you forever."

As he finished with a broad swing of his arms, he suddenly lost his balance and landed in a heap on the carpet. Laughing, he collected himself and added, "I will be careful."

It was now Mollie's turn. She stepped up on the platform. "The idea of the shower was Max's. He is humble and won't want to take the credit, but Mom, I want to tell you it's because of Max that we're doing this. I know you're the best mom in the world. People might think that's true because you have lots of children, but that's not the real reason. I know you are giving years and years of your life to raising us children. It's not always easy or fun. Even if we go on a trip, you still take care of us. You're never on vacation! You know this is what Jesus wants you to do.

"You set a big example with how you live your life. You love to read your Bible, spend time with Dad, with us children, and you let us get Maple. It's been a lot of work to be expecting twins. I know they must be heavy! You never com-

. . . she jumped off the platform and handed Mom the rose.

plain about the nights you can't sleep because the twins are moving around too much, or they are poking you in your ribs. You faithfully prayed for Grandpa and Grandma to accept Jesus as their Lord and Savior.

"We children calculated several interesting facts we'll share. We found that Mom has made over 4,500 dinners, changed over 9,000 diapers—and you'll be adding greatly to that number soon—taught over 1,500 days of school, did Dad's laundry over 1,320 times, and has been pregnant or nursing for at least 2,800 days—that's amazing, Mom! I love you!"

Mollie hopped off the platform and gave Mom a hug. Mrs. Bagwell handed Mom a tissue. "You need it, Emily," she commented.

Max was the final one to share. "Mothers are very important. Without our mothers, we wouldn't be here. I found it interesting as I studied my Bible and discovered that when Jesus tells us to honor our fathers and mothers, which is the fifth commandment, it's also the only commandment with a promise. If we honor our parents, it will go well with us. I desire to always obey you and Dad. Thank you, Dad and Mom, for choosing to let the Lord Jesus give you the number of children He wants to give you. It's not easy, and I don't understand all the hardships that go into being a parent. But, one purpose in marriage is to raise up godly children, which you both—" Max tried to ignore a disturbing sound, which he realized was the noise of wood breaking under his feet. He continued, ". . . are doing. Thank you, Mom, for investing in us." Mr. Delome's camera flashed and startled Max. "I'm also grateful for everyone—" Suddenly, the platform gave way, and Max tumbled to the ground. "Oh well, Grandpa. It lasted almost until the end."

Mr. Delome let out a hearty chuckle, flashing his camera again. "Really, Oliver," Mrs. Bagwell scolded, "you shouldn't get a picture of him like that. If you have one of those digital deals, you could erase it."

"I do, but the picture turned out wonderfully! You don't mind do you, Max?"

"No; it's fine! Mom can now open her gifts."

Maddie carried Mrs. Bagwell's gift to Mom. Mom admired the gift. "What a beautifully wrapped box, Mrs. Bagwell; I couldn't dream of doing this kind of job." Mom gently opened the paper and found two baby sleepers, two pairs of socks, and two yellow bath towels. "Thank you! The sleepers are so cute, and the babies will need socks. The baby towel I have is quite worn, and two will be the perfect thing. Thank you!!"

Grandpa and Grandma gave an activity play gym that the twins could lie under, and Grandma Clifton's gift was a diaper pail with several packages of diapers. Next, Dad gave Mom a baby sling she had wanted. "I will definitely make good use of this! Thank you, Jim!"

Then, the long-anticipated time had arrived: the Moody children's present. They had put their money together and prayed about what gift they could give their mom and the twins. "Here is our present." Mitch brought a medium-size package over to Mom.

"Maddie, would you like to help me?"

"Yes, ma'am." Maddie tore into the paper, and Mom gasped.

"The diaper bag I've been wanting! Oh, children, this is very special."

Mitch couldn't wait any longer. "Dad took us shopping this week, and the bag was on sale. We children had been praying for the right gift, and when we went to the store, we couldn't believe what a good price the bag was. It would have been too expensive before. We were delighted by God's answer to our prayers."

Mom examined the diaper bag, checking out the different compartments and pockets. "It looks sturdy, and it's perfect for what we'll need for the twins."

Maddie watched quietly, but then she interjected. "I can carry it 'round for you and Dad," she offered.

"That would be nice, Maddie."

Mr. Delome had requested his present to be saved until the end. Mitch pulled the gift over near Mom. "Hmmmm," Mom remarked. "I can't figure out this one."

Mr. Delome beamed. "Just tear the paper open from the top," he instructed. He whipped his camera to his eye in anticipation.

Mom followed Mr. Delome's instructions and then stopped, realizing the enormity of the gift. "Mr. Delome! Did you really?" Her eyes sparkled as she saw the front of the large box showed a picture of a twin stroller.

Mitch gazed in wonder. Mr. Delome—who was extremely careful with his money—had purchased the Moody twins a nice stroller! Mr. Delome's camera clicked as he took another picture. "I've never shopped the baby section of a store, but I managed to find my way around. I saw the stroller and knew that was my gift."

"Thank you, Mr. Delome. We will use this frequently, and it'll be such a blessing to be able to push both babies in one stroller!"

"I'll even put it together for you, Mom!" Mitch exclaimed.

Grandma and Mollie left the room to finish final preparations on the dessert. Soon, everyone was called into the dining room. "We're going to do this like a wedding," Mollie shared. "Dad and Mom, you may cut the cake when you're ready." A long knife, with silver etching on the handle, lay beside the cake. "Grandma let me borrow her special cake-cutting knife."

"Mollie! Where did you buy this cake?" Mom wondered. Yellow piping was around the edges, and the middle read, "Welcome, Moody Twins!" Baby "toys" were tastefully drawn on the cake.

"Actually, Mom, that's what Grandma and Maddie and I did this afternoon. We made it!"

"It's beautiful, Mollie. It's so professional looking; I thought you purchased it."

Dad and Mom cut the cake, and Grandma sliced pieces for the guests. Max served ice cream, and Mitch ladled the punch from a crystal bowl. Everyone enjoyed chatting as they ate the dessert. Mr. Delome shook his head. "Mrs. Clifton gave the most useful gift. That diaper pail is huge."

"Do you know whose job it is to empty it?" Mitch asked.

"I seem to remember a young man mentioning that in his 'I wills' speech," Grandpa remarked.

Mitch laughed. "Yes, that's me. I don't mind; it's good experience for if I'm a father someday; that's what Dad told me."

Mr. Delome prepared to leave, and he shook Dad's hand. "I really appreciate your children, Jim. Max, Mollie, Mitch,

Maddie, tonight was really special. I understand why ladies like to go to baby showers. See you later!" With a wave, he was gone.

By the time all of the guests had left, it was ten o'clock, and the Moodys were sitting in the living room discussing the evening. Mom sat in her rocking chair, placing her hands on her large stomach. Tears again rolled down her cheeks. "Are you okay?" Mollie knelt beside Mom with concern.

Mom smiled. "Oh yes; these are happy tears. I can't believe what you did for me. I had not a clue in the world; I feel very loved and blessed. Thank you doesn't seem enough."

Max knelt on the other side of Mom's chair. "Mom, we can never repay you for all you've invested in us. A shower is just a small thing we can do to bless you!"

Dad pulled his Bible out. "You children did an incredible job. I know everyone's tired, but it's important we finish the evening with our family Bible time. We're in Acts 4 tonight."

Chapter 7

A Profitable Birthday

The next morning, Mollie woke with a start. *Today is Dad's birthday. I wonder if the twins will come.* She was glad that they had been able to give the shower before the twins' birth. Mollie threw back her covers, picked an outfit, grabbed the birthday decorating tub from under her bed, and slipped out of the room, allowing Maddie to sleep a little longer. She changed in the bathroom, then knocked softly on the boys' bedroom door and opened it. Maple, who had been sleeping on the floor, perked up her head. Mollie whispered: "Boys, are you awake?"

"Now I am," Mitch mumbled. "Why are you up early on a Saturday morning? Remember, this is our sleep-in morning, and we went to bed late last night!"

"Have you forgotten this is a special day? It's Dad's birthday!" Mollie exclaimed.

Mitch lifted his head. "Yes, I had forgotten." He stretched and looked at Mollie over the bunk-bed railing.

Max slowly sat up. "I was really sleeping well. Are we going to decorate for Dad?"

"I thought it would be nice," Mollie said. "I'm going downstairs to have my time with Jesus. Mom put a note on the bathroom counter, and I saw it when I was getting dressed. Her note requested that we make breakfast, which will be scrambled eggs, biscuits from cans, and hash browns. Maple, c'mon girl. Do you want to go outside?" Mollie motioned to Maple.

Mollie made her way down the stairs, opened the back door, and breathed deeply. The air was crisp, and sunlight was hitting the trees. She looked at the thermometer. *Hopefully it'll warm up today.*

She went into the living room and settled in Dad's chair with her Bible, flipping it open to First John 2. After a half hour, the boys came down, with Maddie trailing behind. "See Maddie? She's right there praying." Max pointed to Mollie.

Maddie's face shone, and she ran for Mollie. "I missed you. Can you help me pick out what I should wear today?"

"I'd love to," Mollie ran her fingers through Maddie's blonde curls.

"Mollie, do you need onions cut up?" Max wondered.

"Yes. Mom usually melts some butter in a pan and then fries the onions. We can use the little grinder instead of hand-chopping the onions."

"I can do that." Max glanced at Mitch. "How about you start with the balloons?"

"May I blow up thirty-six, for Dad's age?"

"I don't know if we have that many," Max observed. "Besides, Mom wouldn't be thrilled with thirty-six balloons lying around!" Max went to the pantry and found the onions. He began peeling the outer, white layer of the three they would use. Mollie came back from helping Maddie and located the electric skillet. She plugged it in and plopped a chunk of butter on the smooth surface, while Max started the grinder. "I'll be fine here in the kitchen, Mollie, if you'd like to decorate. Mitch doesn't enjoy doing the streamers; I know he prefers the balloon part."

"I want to do streamers! Thanks." Mollie skipped out of the kitchen.

Max dumped the contents of the grinder onto the frying pan and used the non-metal spatula to spread the onions around. He checked the temperature on the pan before leaving the room to observe the decorating team.

Mitch's cheeks appeared to be close to bursting while he puffed out and blew up another balloon. Max felt a little concerned as he noticed how many Mitch had already done. "Are you really doing thirty-six, Mitch?"

"No, I was only going to do twenty. I don't know if I'll have enough breath to finish! To think that these balloons have my own breath in them. Oh, what do I smell? Are you burning something?" Mitch scrunched up his nose.

"I hope not. Don't you like onions?"

"Yes, but those are pretty powerful."

Max went back to the kitchen and dumped the frozen hash browns into the pan. *I love to please Dad,* Max thought. *You know, if I enjoy blessing Dad this much, how much more I should love pleasing my Heavenly Father. He sees everything I do. My desire should be to please Jesus all the time!*

Soon, the house was decorated and breakfast almost finished. The children heard Dad's heavy footsteps coming down the stairs. "What a surprise!" Dad beamed. "I didn't know I was going to have this special treatment."

All four children dove for him and shouted, "Happy Birthday!"

"Thank you! Everywhere looks very nice, and breakfast smells good."

"Did the twins comed yet?" Maddie clutched Dad's legs, peering around to see Mom behind him.

"Not yet," Mom patted her stomach. "They're still here and doing well."

At breakfast, Dad asked Mom what they could do to prepare for the twins. "I know we need to get the baby clothes from

"Did the twins comed yet?" Maddie clutched Dad's legs, peering around to see Mom behind him.

the basement. I'm sorry I haven't done that sooner," Dad apologized.

"It's really fine, Jim. I have several sleepers and gowns to start them in, so I wasn't concerned."

"I know what you'd really like," Dad prompted her. "I suppose you want under the bed vacuumed."

Mom giggled. "I wasn't going to say that, but how'd you know?"

"I knew."

Mitch was puzzled. "I don't understand. No one can see under the bed unless they're on the ground."

"That's true, but when I have a baby, I like to know that it's all clean under my bed. It's silly, yet I am just that way. Dad has a great memory."

After breakfast, the family trooped upstairs to Dad and Mom's bedroom. Max carried the vacuum. "How are we going to do this, Dad?"

"The best way is to move the bed over a bit, but that won't work with the new changing table. We'll need to use the wand attachment from the vacuum. You or Mitch could reach under the bed with the wand."

"Jim?" Mom asked when Dad had completed the instructions.

Dad turned around. "Yes?"

"Would you also clean my bedroom window?" Mom's voice carried a small plea. "I'll soon be looking out it a lot."

Dad pondered the window with a twinge of remorse. He wished they had bought a new one that was easier to clean.

But, it wasn't on their priority list of things to purchase. He chuckled. "Sure. Mollie, you can work on the inside. Max and I'll do the outside. Mitch and Maddie, you can clean under the bed."

The phone rang, and Mom answered. "Hello . . . Oh yes, Jaynee . . . We're very blessed, but how are you? . . . No twins yet. Jim and the children are doing cleaning projects for me . . . Yes, it happens every baby. Jim is gracious and knows it's important to me . . . How is your ministry?" With that, Mom stepped out of the room, realizing it would be quieter if she could talk elsewhere.

Mitch was disappointed. "I was hoping to hear the rest of Mom's conversation!"

"Come on now, Mitch," Dad shook his head. "You wouldn't want to eavesdrop; Mom will tell us later. Max, let's get the big ladder and also some cleaning supplies."

Mollie began on the inside of the window while Mitch and Maddie started the job of cleaning out under the bed and vacuuming. Suddenly, a muffled laugh was heard. Mollie glanced in the direction of the laugh. Mitch's legs were sticking out from under the bed, and he was casting unknown objects to Maddie. Giggling, Maddie caught several of the items. "Are you about done?"

"Not quite!" Mitch continued tossing small things out.

"What ARE you finding?" Mollie wondered.

Maddie's small fists were full of Mitch's hunt. "This is a pen," Maddie showed Mollie, "and a big child school 'racer—wonder how that got there?—this is my SOCK!" Maddie became excited. "My fav'wite sock! I did losed it a long time ago." She promptly sat down and pulled off one of her current socks. "Oh no!" she tugged the sock harder, but the heel only hit half way on her foot. "It shrinked!"

"Now," Mitch scooted himself out from under the bed. "I'm through. That was quite a lot of stuff! How old are you, Maddie?"

"I'm four."

"Four years' worth of lost stuff under the bed. We're set to vacuum."

Soon, Dad was on the ladder washing the outside of the window. Maddie waved to Dad and held Mitch's objects up. "Maddie," Mitch decided, "you can dust the head and footboards while I vacuum." When the vacuuming was done, Mitch tackled the spider webs in the corners.

"Since I'm finished with the inside of the window, I'll give Mom's bathroom a thorough cleaning. She can't bend over to clean the shower anymore." Mollie turned to Maddie. "You can help me. Let's gather our supplies."

The girls located what they needed. Maddie carried a squirt bottle filled with water and a rag while Mollie brought the other cleaning equipment. Dad and Max came back in. Dad inspected the window in the light. "It looks pretty good. I wonder what else needs to be finished. We'll do some rearranging since Mom would like her rocking chair in here."

Mollie sprayed the countertop thoroughly and hung the squirt bottle on a loop of her apron. "I hope we have two girls. Can we name them Martha, after Grandma, and Mary?"

"We would continue the 'M' tradition with your idea, wouldn't we?"

Mom walked into the room. "Did I hear Mary and Martha? Those are cute. Dad and I have been talking about baby names. We need to have several sets of names: if we have two boys, two girls, or a boy and a girl. I believe it's going to be two boys. They've been quite active."

Mitch's face lit up. "YES! I have some name suggestions. I've been reading in the Old Testament. Melkizi, Melkeze—"

Max suggested, "Melchizedek?"

"Yes, exactly. That man was a priest, plus Methuselah, Mordecai—not Haman, but that doesn't start with an 'M' anyway—that reminds me." Mitch took a breath before continuing. "I really, really like the name Uriah! Dad, I just read about him in my devotions the other day. He was such a godly man; he was very brave and obeyed King David. Can we name a baby Uriah?"

Dad was thoughtful. "What else did you learn about Uriah?"

"He was very loyal, because when all the men were out fighting, he didn't care about comforts such as being at home. Then, I can't imagine how he felt when all the other soldiers pulled away from him in the heat of the battle. He stayed true to King David all the way to the end."

"I think we can consider Uriah for a middle name, but we'll stick with 'M' for the first name. Emily, should we tell them what we are leaning toward for names?"

Mom had been admiring her clean window. "I think we should."

"Let's do it at lunch."

Chapter 8

Lunch Visitor and the Party

Lunch was simple, since they would be having a big birthday meal for dinner. "I'll make your birthday dessert when we're through with cleanup," Mom remarked to Dad.

"Emily," Dad said, "I really do like Cream Puff Pie, but maybe with you being so close with the twins, it'd be much easier on you for me to swing by the store and pick up some ice cream."

Mom didn't hesitate. "If you're okay with me doing it, I'd really enjoy making the pies. Mollie will help, and it won't take us long."

"Then we will continue as planned," Dad decided. "You're sweet and unselfish. I am continually blessed by you." Everyone gathered at the table, Dad prayed, and then he said, "We've had many discussions about baby names. Mom and I've been praying and seeking the Lord for the right names for the twins. I know you are anxious to hear what we've chosen—taking all possibilities into consideration," Dad looked at Mitch with a hint of a smile in his eyes. "If we have two boys, we like Matthew and Moses. If we have two girls, we like Melody and Missie. If we have a boy and a girl: Moses and Melissa. We haven't decided on middle names yet."

"That's 'citing!" Maddie squealed, leaning over Mitch's arm for the cheese plate. Maddie's action caused Mitch to spill the glass he was setting down, and the liquid moved rapidly in Max's direction.

"Watch it, Max!" Mitch shouted—but it was too late. Max saw the mini-fountain pouring into his lap, and he jumped from his chair as the water splashed onto the floor.

Maddie slipped from her chair and ran over to Max. She started dabbing his jeans with a slightly soggy napkin. "I'm really sorry 'bout that, Max."

"That's fine, Maddie."

Just then, the doorbell rang. Mom laughed. "I guess Max won't be answering the door."

Mitch flew from the room to grab several rags while Max hurried upstairs to change. Dad found Mr. Delome at the door and invited him to join them. "We had a little water spill, but Mitch is taking care of it," Dad explained.

"At least it wasn't pancakes," Mr. Delome said, remembering back to when he had come over several months before and a sticky plate of Maddie's pancakes had been on the floor.

"Are you hungry?" Dad asked. "We're finishing lunch, and you're welcome to join us."

"No, thanks; I already ate," Mr. Delome shook his head.

A few minutes later Max returned. "Hello, Mr. Delome."

"Hi, Max. Now that you're here, I can share the reason I came over. I wanted to tell you children what a splendid job you did on the twins' shower. I really enjoyed myself, and I thought your speeches were superb."

"What's that strange word mean?" Maddie tugged on Mr. Delome's sleeve. He looked down at the blue-eyed, curly-haired girl.

"I guess it means it was more than great! Splendid!"

"What's splendid?" Maddie examined her section of tangerine, trying to decide if it contained seeds. She popped the tangerine into her mouth and then handed Mr. Delome her last wedge. "It's for you—watch out for seeds."

Mr. Delome hesitated slightly but then accepted the offered fruit from the sticky hand. "Thanks, Maddie; you're kind to share. You've got me in a box trying to explain myself. Splendid means it was double great."

"I don't see you in a box," Maddie honestly noted.

"OH!!!" Mr. Delome sounded slightly frustrated. "I guess I'll have to be careful what I say."

"That's okay," Maddie assured him. "I won't ask you any more. Do you know it's my daddy's bifday, I mean bir-rrrthday? I'm sad 'cause those twins still haven't comed."

Mr. Delome nodded at Dad. "Happy Birthday! What have you done this morning, and what are the plans for the rest of the day?"

"The children made a wonderful breakfast and decorated the house. We also cleaned for Emily. She likes to have everything in order before a baby comes. We're going to unearth baby things from the basement this afternoon," Dad told him.

"And," Maddie added, "we're going to do a birthday party. I really like birthday parties. The last one was mine and Mommy's. Do you like birthday parties?"

"Yes, I do."

"We'd love to have you over tonight," Dad offered. "We're going to eat dinner at 5:30, after that we'll have our family Bible time, and then we'll open presents and eat dessert. But, if you come, please don't bring a present, your company is enough."

Mr. Delome rubbed his beard. "I don't have any plans, and I'd like to join you. This probably sounds strange for an old man to say, but you make me feel loved. My family was not like this, and I've come to see that you all are a real family. You're the family I never had—I really mean it." He paused, as if to regain his composure, and continued, "Well, I'd better be off. I have a few errands downtown."

After lunch cleanup, Mom and Mollie worked on the pies while the boys brought several boxes from the basement. Mollie glanced over the recipe.

Cream Puff Pie

(Adult supervision encouraged.)

Yields: 2 pies
1 cup water
½ cup butter
1 cup flour
¼ tsp. salt
4 eggs

Heat oven to 400°F. Grease 2 glass pie pans. In small sauce pan, heat water and butter to rolling boil. While stirring, add in flour and salt. Stir vigorously over low heat about 1 minute or until mixture forms a ball. Remove from heat; put mixture into large bowl and beat in eggs, all at one time, until smooth. Spread smooth in **bottom only** of pie pans. Bake 35-50 minutes (depending on your oven) or until outside edges are puffed and golden. Let cool.

Filling

2 big boxes (6 serving size), instant vanilla pudding
6 cups milk
12 ounces Cool Whip

Mix pudding with milk and beat according to directions on the box. Then, add the Cool Whip. Mix, then pour or spoon into crusts. Chill several hours or ideally overnight before serving.

———————————————

"I don't remember making these before. Are they hard?"

"Not really. You have to follow the directions carefully, but we should do that on each recipe we make." Mom measured the water and butter and put them in a pan on the stove. "We'll wait for it to boil."

Mollie placed a cup of soft white flour next to the stove. Mom cracked four eggs into a bowl. The water and butter came to a boil, and Mom turned the heat down. Mollie added the flour and salt as Mom vigorously stirred until it formed a ball.

"We'll beat in the eggs," said Mollie as she poured the eggs into the pasty-white dough and then turned on the small hand-mixer.

"This looks interesting, Mom! Did we do everything right?" Mollie apprehensively eyed the yellowish, gooey mixture.

"Yes; it's just right," Mom affirmed.

As Mollie spread the batter into two pie pans, Maddie raced into the room, holding up a toy. "I remember this, Mommy!" Her face showed delight. "Now the twins can play with it. May I give it to them after they're borned?"

Mom smiled. "I'm afraid they'll be too young for that. Let's wait until they're a few months old."

When the piecrusts were in the oven, Mom and Mollie joined the rest in the living room. Dad was sorting through

"Maple!" Mom suddenly exclaimed as she caught sight of Maple sitting in the corner with a baby toy in her mouth.

the contents of the boxes, and baby toys were strewn across the floor. Mitch demonstrated how a toy worked. "This was a neat one; I didn't like to share it with Max."

"How can you remember? You were a little guy then." Max wasn't convinced.

"I have a good memory," Mitch declared.

Mollie was going through a neatly stacked pile of baby clothes. "Mom, we have a lot more for girls than boys," Mollie remarked.

"That's possible. We'll have to do clothes shopping if we have two boys."

"Maple!" Mom suddenly exclaimed as she caught sight of Maple sitting in the corner with a baby toy in her mouth.

Dad tried to keep a straight face as he hurried over to the dog. "Well, Emily, I'm afraid this toy won't be a baby toy anymore. Drop it, Maple." Maple obediently dropped the toy for Dad.

When the crusts were baked and cooled, Mom and Mollie were ready to work on the filling. Mollie found the two pudding packages in the pantry and set them on the counter.

"Let's see," Mom rummaged in the cupboard to find a mixing bowl suitable for what they needed. "This one should hold it all."

Mollie opened the pudding boxes and dumped the contents into a bowl. Mom located a whisk from a drawer, and Mollie brought the milk from the refrigerator. In just a few minutes, the pudding was mixed up.

"Yumm. It smells so good," Mollie sniffed the creamy-vanilla pudding.

"I agree. Okay, now we can add the Cool Whip into the pudding, and mix it with a large spoon. That wooden one would work fine." Mollie used the spoon to fold the Cool Whip into the pudding.

"Good. The last step is to pour the filling into the crusts."

Soon, the pies were done, and Mollie placed them in the refrigerator to chill.

The afternoon passed quickly, and soon Grandpa, Grandma, and Mr. Delome arrived. After dinner, the family moved into the living room. Grandpa and Grandma already had their Bibles, and the boys hunted up the family's Bibles. "Would you like to share with me?" Max offered to Mr. Delome.

"Okay." Mr. Delome seemed a little uncomfortable.

"We're in Acts 5," Dad announced. Pages rustled as everyone located the section.

Grandma said, "I found it! I'm learning where the different books are. Grandpa and I've been racing each other to see who can find a book of the Bible first."

It was Max's night to start. "Dad, may I please give my night to you? Since it's your birthday, I want to."

Dad paused and then accepted. "Thank you, Max. Let's pray. Dear Heavenly Father. I feel overwhelmed tonight by Your blessings. I'm unworthy to be a husband to Emily and father to these six children. Help me stay close to You, Jesus. I pray that You would convict me of sin in my life. As we concentrate on Your Word, I ask that You would show us new insights—may each one come away feeling that You have spoken to them through a verse. In Jesus' Name, Amen."

Dad began to read: "But a certain man named Ananias, with Sapphira his wife, sold a possession. And kept back *part* of the price, his wife also being privy *to it*, and brought a certain part, and laid *it* at the apostles' feet."

"Why didn't he give all the money?" Mitch wondered.

"I have an idea," Grandpa offered.

"Go ahead." Dad suddenly noticed Maddie who was busily whispering to her doll. "Maddie, please put your doll down so that you can listen to our Bible reading."

Maddie obeyed. "Yes, sir. I'm sorry for not paying 'tention."

Grandpa tried to keep a straight face as he continued, "I think the reason Ananias only gave part was because of his selfishness and hypocrisy. He wanted to act like the others and appear to give all the money, but he was being selfish and keeping some back for himself."

Dad agreed. "Good point. He was also being purposefully deceptive, even his wife knew of it. I believe the next verses will also reveal something. Go ahead, Grandma."

"But Peter said, Ananias, why hath Satan filled thine heart to lie to the Holy Ghost, and to keep back *part* of the price of the land? Whiles it remained, was it not thine own? And after it was sold, was it not in thine own power? Why hast thou conceived this thing in thine heart? Thou has not lied unto men, but unto God."

"This shows me," Dad said, "that Ananias was convicted by the Holy Spirit, but he disobeyed the promptings. I've told you children many times how important it is to obey the Holy Spirit. Grieving the Holy Spirit is a serious thing."

When they neared the end, it was Mom's turn on verse forty-one. "And they departed from the presence of the council, rejoicing that they were counted worthy to suffer shame for his name."

Mollie shook her head. "Dad, they were excited that they could suffer! I'm amazed they weren't feeling sorry for themselves and wondering why God had allowed their suffering to happen."

Mr. Delome quietly listened to the conversation. He was surprised at how much input the children gave. *They definitely know their Bibles,* he thought. Mollie read the last verse.

There was a minute of silence before Dad said, "I forgot it's my night to start with my favorite verse. I like the final one. The Christians were daily in the temple and in the houses, preaching and teaching Jesus Christ. I'm convicted about the need to be sharing about Jesus more often to others I'm around throughout the day. A few days ago at my lunch break, I had to run an errand to the hardware store. The middle-age man was very friendly, and I felt the Holy Spirit prompting me to share with him. For a moment, I tried to justify in my mind why I shouldn't: I didn't have time and maybe he wouldn't like it. But, I obeyed the Holy Spirit, and the man turned out to be a fellow believer. It was wonderful! It reminded me of the importance of being willing to share no matter what. I'll go your direction, Grandma."

Grandma flipped the page. "Thanks. I can't tell you how I'm enjoying your family Bible times, Jim. They are so different since Jesus is my Savior. My verse is the one right before yours. Jesus has been working in my life, teaching me to deny myself in little ways. I know I have a long way to go to rejoice over the kind of situation they had there, but my desire is that I'm willing and happy to accept whatever happens."

Grandpa adjusted his glasses. "I chose verse five. Ananias had serious consequences for his sin, and it is an example to the rest of us not to disobey the Holy Spirit. I'm new at listening to the Holy Spirit's voice, but like we've talked about, Jim, if we grieve the Holy Spirit by disobeying Him, He'll prompt us less and less. It's only as we obey that still, small voice, will He bless our obedience by revealing more of Himself and prompting us to do His will. And, it sort of goes in a circle, we'll know more of His will by reading more of His Word!"

"You're right," Dad agreed.

Mollie said, "Mine is also the birthday dad's verse. I can be learning how to witness by watching you and Mom. Then, as I grow older and have opportunities, I'll know how. It can be hard to give out a tract, but I'm working at it. I can also be praying for people who you and Mom are able to witness to."

"I like 34," Mitch decided. "Gamaliel was a good man to stand up for the apostles. I want to be loyal and always be true. Too bad Gamaliel didn't start with an 'M'."

Maddie looked disappointed. "Still those twins don't comed. I've been waiting a long time."

Mom stood up. "You're right, Maddie. Mom has too. My legs are cramping, so I need to move around a bit," she explained.

It was Max's turn. "I'll go with the verse of the night, Dad's. I want to be sharing Jesus. I think it's easy to be lazy when I'm out and not give tracts to people, but if I viewed them as about to fall into a lake of fire, I'd feel a real urgency."

Max turned to Mr. Delome, who waved a hand. "I'll pass."

"My verse is Dad's as well," Mom stood with her hands on her stomach. She paused before continuing. "Sorry, one of the twins kicked. I know these next few months I won't be out in public much, but I will have opportunities on the phone. I can also be praying for others."

"Any offenses or things that haven't been dealt with?" Dad asked. There was silence. "I'm glad to see you've taken care of them already."

Mitch raised his hand. "I have a confession, though."

"And what's that?"

"I love Jesus!" Mitch shouted, while the other children cheerfully joined him.

Dad smiled. "I love Jesus too. Romans 10:9 tells us the importance of confessing Jesus Christ with our mouths. May we always be ready to confess our love for Jesus by our words and our lives. How about we sing 'When I Survey the Wondrous Cross'?"

After the Bibles were put away, Dad opened gifts, and then they ate dessert. Another week had ended for the Moodys; another week of waiting had passed.

Chapter 9

"They're HERE!"

Tuesday morning, March 8th, Mom had a request for Dad. "Jim, would you be able to stay home from work? I think the twins will be born today," she announced.

Dad nodded. "Wow! We are anxious for those babies to arrive. I've already been assured at work it'll be no problem to take the time off, so I'll call and let my boss know."

Following the phone call, Dad glanced at his watch. "I know it feels like a holiday with me being home, but children, go ahead with your normal school schedule today. It'll give you something to do."

"Yes, sir." The time seemed to tick by very slowly while the children followed their morning routine. Mitch worked hard on a math problem until he laid down his pencil and sighed. "I wonder when the twins will come. We haven't seen Mom since breakfast."

"I don't know," Max replied. "We'll keep praying."

A little later, Dad came down. "I decided Mom could use a snack. Anyone else hungry?"

Mollie stopped helping Maddie with her workbook. "Yes, sir, I am! Dad, I'm concerned about Mom. Is she okay?"

"Yes, she's doing really well. We've been in contact with Miss Carolyn, and she'll stop by. Her assistant is going to help with the birth. Miss Carolyn thought Mom is still a while away from having the twins, but she wants to come and see how we're doing. Mom and I decided you may eat lunch with us upstairs. She thought you could bring a blanket to cover the bed so we don't get crumbs all over. We'll call it an indoor, bedroom picnic. Try to figure out something that doesn't require silverware."

Lunchtime came, and sandwiches were prepared. The children carried several plates of food upstairs, and Max knocked on the door. "Come in." Mom was in bed. "I've missed you this morning!"

"We missed you!" Mollie affirmed.

After lunch, Maddie hesitated. "When those twins comin'? I don't want to be taking my nap when they are here. Do I still have to take one, Mommy?" Maddie pleaded.

"Yes, ma'am! You don't want to be tired when they're born later, and you can see them. If they come while you are asleep, Mollie will wake you up. But, I don't think they'll come that soon. You should be safe."

The children gave Mom hugs and left the room. Maddie wanted to take her nap earlier than usual, so Mollie tucked her in and read a short book to help her feel sleepy.

Several minutes later, Miss Carolyn and her assistant arrived, and Max let them in. "Hello! This is my younger cousin, Rachel. She helps me at some of my births. Are you all looking forward to the twins?" Miss Carolyn asked.

"Yes, ma'am, we are," Max said as spokesperson for the children.

A half hour later, Miss Carolyn and Rachel came down. "Your mom is doing well. I expect to be back by this evening, but I'll await your parents' call."

Max, Mollie, and Mitch worked hard on their school while Maddie napped. Around three o'clock, Max decided to fix a snack for Mom. He arranged several slices of cheese and wheat crackers on a plate. Mollie and Mitch followed him up the stairs. Max knocked softly on the door, and Dad opened it. "Thanks, Max. Mom just told me she was ready to eat something."

Mollie woke Maddie up and helped her with a craft project in the living room. Soon, Dad came downstairs. "We've called Miss Carolyn and Grandpa and Grandma. It's important that everyone is quiet and very good tonight. Grandma is bringing dinner. Mom is doing well; keep praying for her and the twins. After they're born, I'll bring you upstairs to see them."

When the doorbell rang, the children were expecting Miss Carolyn. Mitch answered the door, and she greeted him. "Hello again! You're about to become a new big brother! I can't wait to see the twins; have a blessed evening with your grandparents." With a wave, she hurried upstairs and her assistant followed.

"That was a big bag Miss Carolyn's friend had," Maddie said. "What's in it, Mollie?"

"I don't know, but I guess baby things," Mollie decided.

A sharp knock on the door was heard, and then Grandpa poked his head in. "The big night is here!" Grandma came in right behind him.

"I'm glad you came," Max sighed. "It'll make the evening go faster."

"Grandma brought dinner, but I'm afraid we can't eat it yet since it's only 4:30," Grandpa informed. He looked at the children's solemn faces. "Cheer up! We're trusting the Lord to take care of your mom and the twins. I have an idea: we'll do our Bible time. We don't know when the twins will decide to arrive, so let's do the most important thing now rather than later."

The children gathered around Grandpa, who sat on the floor with his back against the couch. After a half hour of reading the Bible and everyone discussing different verses, Grandpa suggested they take a walk. He could tell the children were quite distracted, and he knew being out of the house would pass time. "May we take Maple?" Mitch asked Grandpa.

"Sure."

"Walk, Maple!" At those two words, Maple eagerly pranced over to Mitch, wagging her tail. Mitch snapped the leash onto her collar. "Would you like to walk her, Grandpa?" Mitch offered him the leash.

"I'd enjoy that; thanks, Mitch."

Mollie pulled a light jacket from the closet. "What'd you bring for dinner, Grandma?"

They all stepped outside as Grandma answered, "Burritos and chips. I put the burritos together this morning, when your mom called and said they'd likely need us tonight."

"Does your heart hurt?" Mitch wondered.

"No, it doesn't. I know I didn't have a great diet before, so I'm working at eating more fruits and vegetables. Grandpa and I also exercise together. The days he works, we do it before dinner, and the days he's off, we exercise following our time in the Word. I've lost ten pounds, and the doctor is quite pleased."

Grandpa stopped as Maple watched a squirrel. "Did I ever tell you that my family raised golden retrievers?"

Mitch's eyes brightened. "No, Grandpa; we didn't know that. Please tell us the story!"

"We lived on a farm for many years. We raised goldens to sell as puppies for extra income because the farm didn't make much above our needs. When I was twelve, Dad let me pick a puppy from one of our dog's litters. I was thrilled to have a dog of my own. I named her Goldie; she was such a sweet, gentle dog."

Grandma noticed Grandpa's enthusiasm and remarked, "You know, James, I had always told you I wouldn't let you get a dog, but since I made Jesus my Lord and Savior, I realized that I was wrong to say that. I was being controlling. Will you forgive me?"

"I forgive you. By the grace of God, we've both changed greatly."

"To get a dog or not isn't my decision but yours," Grandma continued. "As a matter of fact, if it would make you happy, it would make me happy."

"Bless you," Grandpa smiled at Grandma.

"So," Mitch almost tripped over Maple, who was intently watching another squirrel several feet away. "Does that mean you're going to get a puppy, Grandpa?"

"Not quite that fast, but I'll pray about it. For the moment, I'll enjoy Maple." Grandpa patted her.

At home, the children helped Grandma with dinner preparations. After the girls set the table, Grandma said the burritos still needed ten more minutes in the oven. Since devotions were done, and the twins hadn't come, Grandpa tried to figure out what he'd do with the children. He decided to tell stories from his childhood, but he could see their thoughts were only one place: on the twins.

Finally, the burritos were hot, and Max carried the pan to the table. Grandpa bowed his head. "Let's pray. Dear Heavenly Father, thank You for this evening. I pray that You would give Emily grace and strength as she goes through having these twins. Please protect her and the babies. Please bless this food Grandma prepared. In Jesus' Name, Amen."

The meal passed with the Moody children hardly saying a word, but Grandpa and Grandma kept conversation going between themselves. Suddenly, footsteps were heard on the stairs, and everyone froze. Dad hurried into the room, calling, "They're HERE!"

All the children jumped up and raced for Dad, hugging him. "Are they really—how is Mom—may we see them—are they boys or girls—what did you name them?" A jumble of questions chorused from the children.

"One question at a time. The twins were born five minutes ago. I will keep it a surprise what they are and their names. Mom is doing incredibly well. In fifteen minutes, you may come upstairs." Dad nodded at Grandpa. "Will you watch the clock?"

"I'll be happy to," Grandpa agreed.

The children decided they would not eat a second helping. "Your burritos are great, Grandma, but I'm in a hurry to clean up dinner so we can see the twins," Mitch apologized.

Several minutes later, Mitch, who was whisking around with a broom, stopped. "I hear a baby crying! Wow, I can't believe this." Everyone listened, and smiles spread across each child's face.

Before another word was spoken, the doorbell rang. "At least whoever it is didn't wake the babies," Mitch laughed merrily.

Grandpa answered the door, and Mr. Delome poked in his head. "Hello everyone!" he greeted. "I wanted to see if everything is okay. I saw a car that certainly wasn't yours or the Moodys."

"Yes, that one is the midwife's," Grandpa simply explained.

Mr. Delome was bursting with curiosity. "The twins, are they here yet?"

"Yes, sir!" Max announced. "We'll be seeing them in just a few minutes. We don't know if they're boys or girls. Dad didn't tell us."

"Congratulations to the whole crew!"

Mr. Delome waved, and the children swiftly finished cleaning up the dinner mess. With two minutes to spare, they gathered around Grandpa, eager for the fifteen minutes to be over. "All right. We can go." Trying not to run, the children scaled the steps in a record amount of time.

Max knocked on the bedroom door, and Dad opened it. They stepped in and stood silently, hardly believing their eyes. Two small bundles were snuggled next to Mom in bed. Quiet instrumental music played, and the room was lighted softly by the bed lamps. Mom's face radiated at the sight of the children. "Come closer and see them," she invited.

They all walked over and stopped at the edge of the bed, as if not sure. "You may get on the bed; it won't bother them."

Since walking into the room, they had only been able to see the bundles and not faces. Now, Max's eyes were focused on two tiny faces: perfect, amazing, and wonderful. He felt his vision become blurry as tears dropped from his cheeks.

Mollie peeked around Max's shoulder and couldn't help taking a deep breath. "Mom," she began but couldn't finish as she too began crying.

Mitch quietly soaked in the sight. "Dad, they're ours!" he exclaimed in wonder.

"Yes, they are. Truly, it's a miracle."

Now, Max's eyes were focused on two tiny faces: perfect, amazing, and wonderful.

Maddie reached out a hand to touch them. "Is it okay, Mommy?" she pushed back a blonde curl, looking for approval.

"Yes, Sweetie. Be very gentle." Maddie placed her hand on one of the babies.

"They're warm! Are they really real?"

"They are."

Max had regained his composure. "I can't tell them apart! Are they both girls?"

Dad smiled. "They look pretty similar, but Miss Carolyn says we should be able to tell them apart soon. Actually, children, we have Moses Uriah here on the left, and Melissa Joy on the right!"

"One of each!" Mitch observed.

Mom laid a hand on Melissa. "Would you like to see her little toes?" Mollie nodded, and Mom unwrapped the bottom of the blanket and showed the children.

"They're tiny!" Mollie marveled.

Mom looked at Grandpa and Grandma. "What do you think?"

Grandma wiped her eyes. "I can hardly say anything; it's so great! Emily, you carried those babies for many months. They're incredible."

Grandpa's eyes were fixed on the twins, and he appeared not to hear the conversation. Mom could tell he was deeply moved. Everyone was so focused on the twins they hadn't noticed Miss Carolyn and Rachel, who were standing to the side. "Miss Carolyn and Rachel, you're welcome to get a bite to eat or have some tea or whatever," Mom offered.

Grandma nodded. "There are several burritos in the fridge."

"Thank you!" Miss Carolyn and Rachel went down to the kitchen.

As soon as Dad picked up Melissa, she began crying. Maddie was concerned. "Grandpa, why is the baby crying? I thought she'd be happy to be here."

Grandpa spoke for the first time since entering the room. "Babies cry, Maddie. She has to get used to her new surroundings."

Dad cuddled Melissa, and she stopped crying. "Who would like to hold the twins?" Dad asked.

Everyone wanted a turn. Mom took a sip of water and enjoyed watching the family's delight. After the children and Grandpa and Grandma had a chance to hold the twins, Dad decided that Mom needed to rest.

"We love you," Grandma said. "Grandpa and I would be delighted to stay overnight if you'd like, Jim."

"I really appreciate it, but the children will be fine. If you could stay until bedtime and then tuck them in, I'd be grateful. I'll pray with them a little later on. Max, you may knock on the door when Grandpa and Grandma have left, and I'll come."

"Yes, sir." The children, Grandpa, and Grandma went to the living room, where excited talk continued about the twins. "I can't believe how small they are," Max remarked.

"Moses and Melissa, what cute names. Jesus gave us a boy and a girl!" Mollie exclaimed.

"I don't want to go to bed," Maddie confessed to Grandma. "I want to stay near the babies."

"You'll be able to see the twins tomorrow," Grandma assured her. "Your daddy and mommy will take good care of them tonight."

Grandpa nodded. "Grandma's right, Maddie. I just remembered—Grandma made peanut butter cookies for dessert. Shall we eat them?"

When dessert was through, Grandpa read to the children. The living room felt cozy as they listened to Grandpa's deep voice. Maple lay contentedly curled up next to Max. Grandpa read several chapters and then announced, "Time for bed." The children went upstairs and prepared for bed. Grandma talked to the girls in their room and Grandpa to the boys.

"Grandma," Mollie fingered her sheets. "What did Grandpa *really* think about the twins?"

"I think he was overwhelmed by them. You probably don't know this but Grandpa and I had never been convinced about children being a blessing before he was a Christian. After Grandpa accepted Jesus, he began thinking and studying different convictions your family has. One area was children. I remember that day when he came and told me that children were clearly God's gift and were to be received from Jesus. I thought he was a little strange but was glad he was happy about your parents having more children. I think when he saw the twins, he was feeling amazed at their perfectness, the awesomeness of God's creation."

Grandma paused and then continued, "You know, girls, you'll have many opportunities to be a blessing to your parents with the twins here. Keep on with your love for God's Word, listening to the Holy Spirit, and obeying Him!" After a few more minutes of chatting, Grandma kissed them and said good night.

Chapter
10

Adjusting to the Change

The next morning, Mollie woke up, and her heart jumped as she thought of Moses and Melissa. *Thank You, Jesus, for the twins,* she prayed silently. She turned on a small lamp and opened her Bible to Philippians 3. Dad had encouraged her to read and meditate on that chapter since she had discussed with him her struggle being thankful and praising the Lord.

Several minutes later, Mollie woke Maddie: "Time to wake up. Remember the twins are here!"

Maddie rolled over and mumbled something. *I guess I'll let her sleep while I have my prayer time in the living room.* Mollie picked an outfit from the closet and went to the bathroom to change. She hurried downstairs to have her prayer time. When she was done, she walked to the kitchen. *Grandma left the kitchen spotless,* Mollie thought. *She must have tidied a few things after she tucked us in bed.*

Just then, Dad appeared. Mollie ran over and gave him a hug. "How are the twins?"

"They are doing well, and they're sleeping at the moment. Mom fed them in the night several times, plus Melissa seemed restless, so Mom and I were up for a few hours. Mom was still tired this morning, and I encouraged her to sleep as long as she could because the twins are both asleep now. Would you like help with breakfast, Mollie?"

"I'd enjoy that; I'm not sure what we should have. Today is normally muffins, but that'd take a while to make. We could eat fruit and bagels. What do you think?"

"Fruit and bagels would be fine."

At breakfast, the children liked having Dad with them. "Why don't you pray this morning?" Dad asked Max.

"Yes, sir. Dear Heavenly Father, thank You for Moses and Melissa. How blessed we are to have them. I pray that Mom would feel better. Please direct us in what we should do today. Thank You for Dad and Mollie's breakfast preparations. Please bless this food. In Jesus' Name, Amen."

Mitch started the conversation, "Did anyone hear the twins cry last night, except for Dad?"

Mollie shook her head, but Max nodded. "I did. The crying didn't last long; at first, it surprised me because I'm not used to hearing a baby cry!"

Max turned to Dad. "What can we do to help you and Mom today?"

Dad seemed pleased. "After we're through with breakfast, I'll see if Mom is awake and nursing the twins. She planned on feeding them when they woke up. I'd be grateful if you'd fix a plate of food, and then when the twins have been fed, we can talk with her while she eats breakfast. I know she's eager to see you!"

Several minutes later, Dad went upstairs. Mollie poured a glass of orange juice, and the boys arranged a bagel and fruit on a plate. They put the items in the refrigerator. Dad came back down and said that they could join him in a half hour. The children did some small cleaning tasks while waiting for the time to go by. "Ready?" Max asked the others.

They followed Max up the stairs, and Maddie knocked on the door. "It's us, Mommy! May we come in?"

"Just a minute," Dad called. Soon, footsteps were heard, and he opened the door.

Mom was sitting in bed, her hair loosely pulled back in a ponytail. She was holding one of the twins. "Which one is that?" Mitch asked, setting a plate next to Mom.

"Melissa. Isn't she sweet?"

"What color eyes does she have?" Mollie wondered.

"She's not kept them open very long," Mom said, "but I believe they're brown. Why don't Mitch and Maddie start with holding the twins?"

Maddie climbed on the bed, her face radiant with excitement. She held out her arms, and Mom carefully gave her Melissa. Mitch settled himself on the bed, and Dad situated Moses in Mitch's arms. Maddie looked in awe at Melissa. "Why her eyes closed?" she wondered.

"She's sleeping," Mom replied.

Dad said, "I've thought over the day's plans. First, we'll be taking two weeks off from school. I'll be home for a while because I'm using two weeks of my vacation time from work to help with the twins.

"This morning would be a good time to call some of our friends and relatives about the twins. Mom and I've discussed the people we think we should personally call, and then we'll send out an e-mail to others later today. For the phone calls, we'll draw names to see who you each will call. I wrote out the names on little slips of paper and put them in this basket.

"I also have to go to the County Health Department to get birth certificates for the twins. Several of you may come although I want to leave someone home with Mom."

Maddie had a request as Dad shook the basket. "May I call Grandpa and Grandma? I don't know about talking to other peoples."

"Great idea," Dad agreed, knowing Grandpa and Grandma would enjoy hearing from Maddie, even though it wouldn't really be "news" to them. "Mitch, you may pick first."

Mitch fumbled around and grabbed a slip. He silently read the printed words: Aunt Olga. His heart quickly sank. "Who'd you get?" Mollie was curious.

"Aunt Olga," Mitch said slowly, and then he burst out laughing. "I like that. She'll be a challenge!"

"Aunt Olga is hard, but I'm glad it worked out that you picked her," Dad encouraged. "We know you have a way of getting through to her that the rest of us can't seem to touch. I didn't put Mom's parents in the basket; Mom will make that call."

"Why don't we see them or have much of a relationship?" Mollie asked a question that was close to Mom's heart.

Dad shook his head. "It's a long story. Mom grew up in a home where she was sent to church on Sunday. But just because Mom went to a church didn't make her a Christian. In fact, that church did not teach that salvation is through Jesus Christ. Mom's parents felt it was good for her to go to church, but they didn't go. It was right before Mom and I married that she accepted Jesus Christ as her Lord and Savior. They were never very interested in our family. They have busy lives into which we didn't seem to fit. Then, five years ago, her dad retired, and they moved to France. We've not seen them since. Mom will once in a while receive an e-mail from them. Mom and I pray for them quite often."

Max's slip was Pastor Thompson, and Mollie's was Uncle Nathan and Aunt Melanie. There were enough slips to pick for two more rounds. "I need some time to think about how I should tell Aunt Olga," Mitch requested. "Go ahead, Mollie."

Mollie flipped through Mom's address book and found Aunt Melanie's number. "It's been quite awhile since we called people when Maddie was born! It's one of my favorite things to do after a baby is born," Mollie exclaimed. "I need to say the babies' names, weight, and what else?"

Mitch prompted, "Make sure to tell their middle names. For some reason people always want that information."

Mollie dialed the number and eagerly waited for an answer. "Hi, Uncle Nathan! This is Mollie . . . Yes, sir. I'm calling to tell you our news. Would Aunt Melanie be able to get on the phone too? . . . Hi, Aunt Melanie! Mom had the twins last night at 8:12 p.m. . . . Their names are Moses Uriah and Melissa Joy. Moses weighed 6 pounds, 6 ounces, and Melissa is 5 pounds 15 ounces . . . Mom is doing extremely well; we're trying to take care of her . . . You're welcome . . . Bye!"

Mollie looked at the boys. "Who's next?"

Mitch shook his head. Max dialed Pastor Thompson's phone number. "Hello, this is Max Moody . . . Yes . . . Maxwell Moody . . . Can you hear me? . . . Yes, I'll do that." Max pushed the phone off. "It sounded like Mrs. Thompson was grinding wheat! Pastor Thompson is going to switch phones and said I should call him back in a minute."

Max re-dialed the number. "Pastor Thompson? Yes, this is Max Moody again . . . That's okay; it did sound pretty loud . . . We wanted to tell you that the twins were born last night . . . Mom had a boy and a girl: Moses Uriah and Melissa Joy . . . They are doing well . . . Yes, sir, let me ask." Max pushed the hold button and turned to Dad. "Pastor Thompson would like to know if the church can bring us meals for several nights."

"That'd be a blessing."

"Pastor Thompson, Dad says that would be a blessing . . . Good-bye!" The phone beeped as Max turned it off and handed it to Mitch. "It's your turn."

Mitch dialed the number. "Hello! Aunt Olga, this is Mitch . . . Yes, Mitch Moody . . . I'm Jim and Emily's SON . . . Right . . . Do you have a minute? . . . I have good news and bad news for you. Which would you like first? . . . The bad news is that you aren't here to see how precious the twins are . . . Yes, well, I haven't told you the good news. Mom had twins last night . . . Yes, ma'am. Twins . . . We think it's double-great news . . ."

When Mitch was through, Mollie made the next call, and the children continued phone calls until they had completed the list. Mitch then asked Mom, "May we help you with anything?"

Mom stroked Moses' cheek. "Miss Carolyn encouraged me to stay upstairs in my room and rest for a week. Dad and Miss Carolyn feel it's the best thing for me."

Dad nodded. "Right. I could use some helpers to run the house. Maybe Mitch can even give me a lesson on how to clean the bathroom! It's time for Mom to feed the twins so they can nap."

"Yes, sir." Max and the other children left the room. "Let's go down to the living room," Max encouraged. "I have an idea." When they had gathered there, he continued: "Do you remember when Maddie was born, and we made a sign and taped it on our mailbox that said 'It's a girl'?"

"Oh yes," Maddie agreed. "I do. It was pink and had balloons."

Mitch laughed. "Maddie, you were just like the twins. You wouldn't remember."

Maddie looked confused. "I thought I remembered it."

"You probably saw a picture," Mollie smiled warmly at Maddie. "I know, Max. We could write 'It's the twins,' or 'They're here—a boy AND a girl.'"

"The only problem is we don't have any of that poster board paper," Mitch decided. "I wonder if Grandpa would take us to the craft store to get some."

"We need to ask Dad first," Max said. "I think he might be down in a few minutes."

Before long, Dad walked in. "Looks like a planning meeting," he stated.

"We wondered if we could ask Grandpa to take us to the craft store to get some poster board for a sign for the mailbox. Is that okay with you?" Max asked.

"Yes. You may go if Grandpa can take you."

Max called Grandpa and soon came back announcing Grandpa had approved of the plan. The children hurried to get ready.

Grandpa came within fifteen minutes. "I was hoping you would need me for *something*. I know all the excitement is over here, and it's too hard to sit home, especially because I didn't have to go to work today. Grandma joined me. She wanted to see the twins again, and if your mom needs to nap, she brought some reading material."

Grandma carried a basket. "I made banana bread, and I thought you might like some."

The errand was uneventful, and Grandpa called Dad to see if he could take the children to lunch. "Your dad said it was fine, as long as Maddie's home by two for her nap," Grandpa informed them. After lunch, Grandpa drove the children home. They all went in the house and found Grandma talking with Mom and Dad in the bedroom. Grandpa peeked at the twins, and then he and Grandma headed home. Mollie tucked Maddie in for a nap, and then they worked on the sign.

By mid-afternoon, the sign was ready to be placed on the mailbox. "I'll wake Maddie," Mollie offered.

"Sure," Max agreed. "She would want to join us."

Soon, Maddie was up, and the children went outside for the event. "It's pretty warm today," Mitch commented.

Mollie and Mitch held the sign while Max duct-taped it to the mailbox. "It's crooked," Maddie offered, her head tilted to one side, squinting from the sunshine.

Max tried not to laugh at Maddie's funny appearance as he made a small adjustment. "How does it look now? Try holding your head straight."

Maddie stood tall. "It's good."

The sign had turned out well.

The sign had turned out well. They had chosen a piece of light yellow poster board, and Max had written "Twins! A Boy and A Girl!" and then at the bottom "Lo, children are an heritage of the LORD . . . Psalms 127:3." Just then, someone honked his horn and slowed down.

They recognized the driver to be the man they had caroled to whose mother had died last year. "Hi, children! I see from the sign that your mom had twins; that's neat. What did you name them?" he asked.

"Moses Uriah and Melissa Joy," Max replied.

"I like those names! Congratulations to the family!" With that, the man waved and drove off.

Mr. Delome, who had been waiting all day for an opportunity to talk to the Moodys, hurried from his house. "How are Moses and Melissa?"

"They're doing very well!" Max replied. "Grandpa took us to the craft store earlier to get the poster board for the sign, and then I wrote it. Mom is resting today, but we've still seen the twins."

Maddie shaded her eyes from the sun as she watched Mr. Delome. Pointing to her doll stroller, she said, "Those are my twins, just like Moses and Melissa. Do you like them?" she asked Mr. Delome.

"Yes, but what are their names?"

Maddie was quiet. "I don't know; I haven't named them yet."

Dad came out, announcing it was time to go to the Health Department. The children said good-bye to Mr. Delome and went inside. "I'll stay home and help Mom," Mollie eagerly offered.

"Me, too," Maddie chimed. "I'll just sit in the corner."

"Okay. The boys and I will be the errand runners."

Dad took the girls up to Mom's room. Mom was sitting in bed, with her Bible open. She smiled at them. "Hello! I've missed you."

Mollie felt a fresh sense of awe looking at the tiny babies, snuggled next to each other. "Do they wake easily?"

"They seem to be pretty sound sleepers right now. If one grunts, the other will often do the same thing. It's sweet."

Dad kissed Mom. "We're going to get the birth certificates taken care of. Do you need anything at the grocery store?"

"I don't think so—Mollie, is our milk holding out?"

"Yes, ma'am."

"Don't forget," Dad reminded Mom. "The Browns are bringing dinner around five-thirty."

"Thanks, Dear; I would have forgotten."

"Love you all!" Dad waved, walking out the door.

Maddie hurried to her room and brought back her baby dolls. "I'll stay with them over here."

Mom closed her Bible and talked with Mollie for several minutes. Mom yawned. "It's funny how tired I get. Hopefully I'll be able to get more sleep at night before too long." Mollie and Maddie each held a twin for half an hour. Finally, Mom glanced at the clock. "I already took a nap, but I should probably close my eyes for a little while because I'll be up again tonight!"

"That's a good idea, Mom," Mollie said. "I noticed we don't have much bread left. Should I make a batch?"

"That would be wonderful. You know how to grind the wheat, right?"

"Yes, ma'am."

Chapter 11 | Special Things and Growth Opportunities

The next morning, the children slept until 7:15. They were quiet as they had their time in God's Word and then prepared for the day, knowing that Dad and Mom had probably been up with the twins in the night. They were determined to make Mom feel special in every way that they could. Max had suggested making Mom's favorite breakfast.

They all met in the kitchen at eight o'clock. Mollie went to the cupboard and pulled out the cookbook. "Here's the piecrust recipe."

"May I draw something for Mom?" Maddie asked.

"Sure," Max agreed. "Why don't you sit on the floor so you'll be near us?"

Maple padded into the kitchen, and Maddie hugged her. "I like you Maple, but you're not as good as the twins. Do you want to eat?" Maple perked up her ears. "Come on," Maddie invited as Maple followed her into the back room. It had become Maddie's responsibility to feed Maple three times a day.

Max mixed up the piecrust while Mitch made Mom's favorite juice: cranberry-apple from frozen concentrate. Mollie peeled and sliced two oranges. "Are we going to give Dad the same breakfast?" she wondered.

"Oh yes. He likes piecrust as much as Mom does." The Moodys' version of breakfast piecrust was piecrust dough rolled thin, melted butter spread evenly across the top, and then a generous dusting of white sugar and cinnamon, baked crispy in the oven. It was a treat, and they only had it on special occasions.

When Maddie came back from feeding Maple, she settled on the floor with her paper and crayons. Mitch helped Max roll the piecrust dough out and cover it with butter, sugar, and cinnamon. They cut the crust into small rectangular pieces and put them onto cookie sheets and slid the pans into the oven. Soon, the smell of cinnamon piecrust filled the kitchen.

"I'll start some laundry before breakfast," Mollie told the boys as she hurried to the laundry room. With dismay, she found the boys' clothes in the washing machine. *They're supposed to be responsible for their clothes,* she thought. *It's not my job to take care of them.* Suddenly, conviction gripped her heart. She remembered a verse she had memorized. *"Let nothing be done through strife or vainglory; but in lowliness of mind let each esteem other better than themselves"* (Philippians 2:3). She cast the negative thoughts from her mind. *I'll be happy to bless them. I'll even fold their clothes later. I don't think Mom always feels like taking care of us each day.*

When Mollie walked back into the kitchen, Mitch was sitting on the floor, admiring Maddie's picture. "I like your picture, Maddie. Mom will enjoy it."

Just then, Dad came downstairs. "Good morning, children! It smells scrumptious!"

"We're making cinnamon and sugar piecrust," Mitch informed Dad.

"Your mom's favorite," Dad smiled.

A soft knock was heard on the front door. Dad opened it, and Mrs. Bagwell stood there. "Thank you for calling me about the twins yesterday. Congratulations!" she beamed. "I thought I'd bring two baskets over. This one is for the mom, and I thought the children might enjoy a few things as well, little snacks and such."

"You're very kind," Dad gratefully thanked her. "Would you like to step in and see the twins?"

Mrs. Bagwell shook her head. "Yes, but no. I'll give you a few more days to settle into the change. Don't worry; I'll be back to see them!"

The children finished preparing breakfast and arranged a tray for Mom: a glass of milk, a plate of piecrust with a small bowl

The children finished preparing breakfast and arranged a tray for Mom: a glass of milk, a plate of piecrust with a small bowl of orange sections, and Maddie's picture.

of orange sections, and Maddie's picture. Max carried a separate tray for Dad. Mom was thrilled with the special delivery. "You children went to so much work! Thank you! You remembered how I like piecrusts," she exclaimed. The children took turns holding the twins while Dad and Mom ate.

A loud bark was heard outside the bedroom door. "I guess Maple's feeling left out," Dad chuckled. He opened the door. "Maple, you need to go lie down."

"Dad has told me you're doing well keeping the house clean," Mom praised the children. "I've missed being downstairs."

"We're glad to do it." Max was now holding Melissa.

The next several days were filled with helping Dad and Mom, holding the twins when it was possible, keeping the house clean, and whatever other tasks needed to be done. Sunday, Grandpa and Grandma joined the family for a home church service.

Chapter 12

Settling into the New Life

Tuesday, the 15th, rolled around, and Max, Mollie, and Mitch were discussing how to split the morning's work. They knew the house needed a thorough cleaning because Mrs. Bagwell was going to stop by after lunch. Max shook his head. "I have a new appreciation for all Mom does. The house doesn't pick itself up! I'll clean the living room, dining room, and kitchen. Mitch, you can do the back room, laundry room, and bathroom. Mollie, why don't you work upstairs? Oh, that's right, Mitch. The diaper pail needs to be emptied. If any of us gets done earlier, we'll help the other one."

Mollie and Mitch went their separate ways to begin cleaning. Maddie tapped Max's arm. "What can I do?"

"I have a job for you." Max handed Maddie the feather duster. "Do you know how to dust?" he asked.

Maddie nodded, a bright smile enveloping her face. "Mom taught me, and I've watched Mollie do it. I can be the big girl!" She eyed the duster and set off to her job.

A few minutes later, Maddie shouted for Max's attention. He turned off the vacuum and looked in the direction Maddie was pointing. Maple stood, head hanging and tail drooping, with socks sticking out of her mouth.

"Maple," he scolded. "You're not supposed to have those." As he drew closer, Maple let the socks fall from her mouth.

Maddie seemed upset. "Those are Mollie's favorite socks—Maple ruined them."

The pink and white dotted socks showed that Maple had been shredding them with her teeth. Max remembered Dad's rule for Maple: if she damaged or destroyed something, she had to spend a half hour in her plastic kennel. "I'm sorry, Maple; I'll have to put you in your kennel." Maple's tail was tucked as she followed Max to the kennel. "We'll let you out after a while." Max turned back to Maddie. "I thought Maple didn't do things like that anymore. Maybe she's feeling sorry for herself since we're so excited about the twins!"

Mollie came downstairs, cheerfully singing, until she saw the socks. "What happened?" she bent down, and before any response could be given, she exclaimed, "Did Maple chew my socks?"

"I'm sorry. She ripped my favorite jumper one time. But, Mommy fixed it for me. If I had 'nough money, I'd buy you new socks."

Mollie gave Maddie a hug. "It's okay; they're only socks. How is your cleaning going?"

"Good. I'm the duster."

The rest of the morning passed uneventfully. At lunch, Mrs. Johnson, Dad's coworker's wife, called. "Hello, Mrs. Johnson," Max said. "Yes, ma'am. The twins are doing great. They sleep most of the time, but Mom said that's what babies do . . . Dad is off work for two weeks, which has been a blessing . . . The church has brought us several meals, and we children have also made a few . . . I know we're being careful to avoid colds, so thank you . . . Yes, ma'am; I'll tell her. By the way, we've been enjoying that new changing table you gave us. We're grateful for you and your husband blessing us with it . . . Good-bye."

That night, Mom came downstairs for the first time since the twins were born to join the family for dinner. Max, Mollie, and Mitch had prepared a special meal: tacos, salad, and chips. Mom was pleased as she looked around the house. "You children did an excellent job keeping the house tidied!"

Dad clipped the baby monitor to his belt. "Where'd you get that?" Mollie wondered.

"It's a monitor we had since Maddie was a baby. The base unit, which is like a microphone, is in our bedroom, and then I can hear the twins on this." Everyone was quiet listening for baby sounds. "They're sleeping now so they shouldn't make much noise, but if they start to cry, we will know it."

After dinner, Mom pushed back her chair. "I'm hearing Moses and Melissa waking up, and it's time to feed them. Jim, I'll try to get down for part of devotions, but it'll take me a while to feed them. Thank you children again for all you did with dinner. It was wonderful."

"You're welcome," Mollie spoke for the rest.

Dad and the children cleaned up the dinner mess and then gathered their Bibles for devotions. They enjoyed chatting for a few minutes before Dad said, "It's time we start into God's Word. Mitch—your turn tonight."

A half hour later, Mom came downstairs with Moses in her arms. Dad took a break from devotions to go get Melissa. "You all may hold them following devotions," Dad decided.

When the Moodys finished, Dad asked, "How many volunteers do I have?"

Four voices were heard. "If Mom would have had four babies, then we wouldn't have to share!" Mitch said. "I can't remember what they're called—maybe fourlets."

"Quadruplets," Max corrected.

Dad's last week off work passed quickly. One morning, the boys and Dad went grocery shopping, and the girls were in the living room with Mom and the twins. Mom laid out a blanket and snuggled the twins together. "I'm clearly seeing their little personalities. Moses is noisier, and Melissa is pretty quiet. It's cute that they have such different eye colors: Moses' are blue, and Melissa's are brown. They also like to stay close."

"I don't know how we did without them," Mollie sighed. "They're sweet. Are you getting enough sleep, Mom?"

Mom shrugged her shoulders. "I'm working on it. I take naps during the day when I can to make up for the lost sleep. The twins are starting to sleep longer stretches in the night, which is a blessing. Did you know Grandpa and Grandma have offered to come over after Dad goes back to work?"

"Wow! That'll be neat!" Mollie was pleased with the idea.

"It will be a blessing," Mom agreed. "Grandma will be helping with school."

Wednesday morning arrived, and Dad's two-week vacation was over. When Max awakened at 6:15, he felt prompted to get up so that he'd have time to pack Dad a lunch. *I wonder if the Holy Spirit told me to do that.* Then, Max remembered something: he knew it wasn't his flesh wanting him to get up early; it must mean that it was the Holy Spirit. He slipped out of bed, felt for his Bible, and walked carefully to the door. Maple heard him, so she followed. They quietly went to the living room, and Max switched on a lamp. *It feels chilly; I wonder what the temperature is.* He grabbed a blanket, plopped into Dad's recliner, and Maple curled up next to the chair.

When Max was done, he let Maple outside. It was a cool morning but not cold enough to wear a heavy jacket. He turned around and bumped into Dad.

"Good morning!" Max exclaimed.

Dad hugged him. "Good morning, Max. You're awake early."

"Yes, sir. I wanted to get up so that I would have time to make your lunch. Is it hard to go back to work?'

"In a way, yes, but I know it's important and what God has called me to do as your dad. I'm glad I was able to take off two weeks. Adjusting to the twins has gone smoothly, but I know Mom can use the extra help Grandpa and Grandma will give. Last night was pretty rough because Moses was up a lot. Mom thinks what she ate for dinner bothered Moses' stomach. She's a little concerned he might have food allergies because Melissa did just fine. We'll have to see. Mom is tired, so I asked her to take a nap after Grandpa and Grandma get here."

Dad went upstairs, and Max worked on Dad's lunch. He made a turkey and cheese sandwich and wrapped it in plastic. Max found Dad's small cooler and packed the sandwich and an apple in it. Grandma had made brownies the day before, so Max put two pieces in a plastic bag and then placed it on top of the other items. Max penned an encouraging note to Dad and zipped the cooler up.

After Dad left and breakfast was through, a brisk knock was heard, and the front door swung open. "Good morning!" Grandpa's cheerful voice boomed. "We're here." Maple ran for Grandpa, barking loudly. "It's okay, Maple." Grandpa stopped to rub her ears.

"Are you going to get a puppy?" Mitch asked, remembering the recent conversation.

"Not yet." Grandpa hung their jackets in the closet. "It looks like you're cleaning. May I help you with your chores?"

Mitch seemed surprised. "You really want to? I'm doing the bathroom right now. I usually clean it on Friday, but for some reason, it needed it earlier."

Grandpa laughed. "I'll help. I've never cleaned a bathroom before, but Grandma will be happy for me to learn how."

"You're right!" Grandma gave him a playful poke as she walked past. Mom came down the stairs with Moses, who was crying.

"Good morning!" Mom had to speak a little louder due to Moses' noise. "Moses isn't feeling well this morning." She planted a kiss on Moses' forehead.

"I'm sorry, Emily. We'll take care of him," Grandma offered.

"I'm grateful; I'll bring Melissa down, too. First, I'd like to show you the children's new school schedule. I modified it for this next month when I won't have as much time to be involved."

Moses stopped crying as Mom showed Grandma the brightly-colored MOTH schedule hanging on the wall. "Jim and I've been praying about it since the twins were born. We spent yesterday working with the schedule and last night we shared it with the children. Maddie'll be the only one who needs help with it since she can't read."

"We'll follow it, Emily."

"Thank you." Mom handed Moses to Grandma. "I'll run upstairs and get Melissa."

Mom was soon back with Melissa. "She's sleeping, so I'll put her in the bassinet." Mom laid Melissa in a small, portable crib in the corner of the living room. She gently tucked several blankets around Melissa and patted her. "Oh, another thing," Mom paused. "Max and Mollie may hold the babies without having to ask, but Mitch can only hold them if he is sitting down. He can't walk around with them, and Maddie can't hold the twins unless you or Grandpa are right there with her."

"Got it; I hope you are able to nap."

"Thank you. The twins will need to be fed in two hours, so I'll be down to get them."

Around nine-thirty, the children were through with their chores and ready to start school. "I'll watch the twins," Grandpa offered to Grandma. "I can hold Moses. When he falls asleep, does he need to go in the little crib?"

Grandma smiled. "Only if you want."

"I'd rather hold him," Grandpa sheepishly admitted.

Mollie and Maddie brought their schoolbooks to the table while Max and Mitch went to the living room. Grandma looked at the schedule and then decided, "While you children start school and Grandpa watches the twins, I'm going to cut vegetables for soup."

A little while later, Mitch's mind was filled with a hard division problem when a clicking noise and several other odd sounds made him look in Grandpa's direction. "Good boy," Grandpa said, smiling at Moses. Grandpa realized Mitch was watching him, and he grinned. "I hope I don't wake up Melissa. I can't hold two at a time."

"You won't; Melissa is a pretty sound sleeper."

In the dining room, Mollie's school was not without struggles. Tears began dropping down her cheeks and splashing onto her paper. Maddie quietly slipped from her chair and went into the kitchen. "Grandma, Mollie is sad. Can you come?"

Grandma found Mollie with her head in her hands. "What's the matter, Sweetie?"

"This math lesson's hard. I've tried and tried and tried, and I can't figure out what they're teaching me. Usually Mom helps, but she can't." Mollie began sobbing.

"It's okay; I'll help you." Grandma flipped the page over and skimmed the lesson. Within a few minutes, Mollie's tears were dried, and she was again working.

Mitch decided his pencil needed sharpening, so he stood up, and on his way to the dining room, he peeked out the front window. "I guess there's no school today," he remarked.

"Why is that?" Mollie wondered.

"I saw two children riding their bikes down the street. I didn't recognize them. Maybe they live up a cul-de-sac."

Grandma found Mollie with her head in her hands.

Chapter
13

The Accident

Melissa awoke and began fussing. "Martha," Grandpa called. "Would you please help me?" Grandma hurried in, and Grandpa handed sleeping Moses to her. He picked up Melissa from the bassinet while Grandma cuddled Moses.

Max closed his English book. "Well, that's done for today. Aren't the twins cute, Grandpa?"

"Yes, they are." Grandpa noticed Mom coming down the stairs. "Were you able to sleep?"

"I was. Thanks for helping with the twins; how'd they do?"

"Melissa just woke up, and Moses has been asleep for about an hour."

Maddie hopped around behind Grandpa, trying to get Melissa's attention. "I'll make Melissa happy, okay Grandpa?"

"Okay."

After a minute, Maddie wondered: "Why doesn't she smile at me?"

Grandpa shrugged. "She's too young, although it's been so long since I've been around babies, I'm not sure when she would begin to smile. Emily, what do you think?"

"They'll probably start in a few weeks," Mom said.

Just then, a muffled scream was heard, and it was obviously not coming from inside the Moodys' house. "What was that?" Grandpa hurried to the window. "Oh no!" he gasped.

Grandpa quickly gave Melissa to Mom and sprinted for the front door with Max, Mollie, and Mitch close behind. A young boy sat in the street near Grandpa's truck, crying loudly. His bike was lying behind Grandpa's pickup truck. "Are you okay, Joey?" A girl, who appeared to be his sister, knelt next to him.

"Maybe, but my head hurts!"

Grandpa ran to the children and quickly looked at Joey to see if his injuries required immediate medical attention. A bump was growing over the little boy's eye, and otherwise he appeared fine. *Thank You, Jesus, for keeping this boy safe,* Grandpa silently rejoiced. Joey stood up. "I'm really fine, Mister."

"Good," Grandpa said. "Why don't you sit on our driveway so you'll be out of the street? You also look cold." Joey obediently walked over to the driveway while Grandpa unbut-

His bike was lying behind Grandpa's pickup truck.

toned his flannel shirt and wrapped it around the shivering boy. He turned to the little girl. "Where do you live? I'll call your parents."

"We live down there and then you turn that way," the girl pointed several different directions. "It's hard to describe where, but I know my phone number. I don't have a dad anymore."

Grandpa dialed the mother's number with his cell phone. "Yes, ma'am. My name is James Moody, and your children had a minor bicycle accident in front of my son's house . . . Don't worry, ma'am . . . Yes, they live at 24 Strawberry Lane." Grandpa took the phone away from his ear. "I guess she hung up."

Both children sat next to each other on the driveway. "Mister," the little girl seemed nervous, "I'm really sorry Joey smashed into your truck."

"I understand; the truck should be fine."

Mr. Delome hurried across the street. "I saw the whole thing, but my son called just then, otherwise I would've been out sooner."

"Mom's not going to like this," the girl observed. "She wanted us to wear helmets, but we didn't!"

Soon, an old car pulled up, and a woman jumped out. She jogged over to them. "Oh, Joey! Are you hurt?" When he didn't respond, she turned to Grandpa. "Is that your truck?"

"Yes," Grandpa answered.

The woman continued, "You should not have parked in the street. It's entirely your fault," she said angrily. She took her children's hands as if to leave.

Sirens were heard, and everyone watched as a police car sped toward them. "Someone must have called the police," Mitch remarked.

"It wasn't me," Mr. Delome whispered.

A policeman jumped from the vehicle. "Anyone hurt?"

Joey shook his head. "I'm fine; just a little bump on my head."

The officer glanced at Joey and seemed satisfied. "I'll cancel the ambulance." He spoke into the radio that was clipped on his shoulder. After he was through, he turned back to the group. "I'm Officer Downing. What happened?" Mitch recognized Officer Downing to be the young officer who had responded to the bank alarm last month. Officer Downing had been the one to reassure Mitch when the door had slammed behind them.

Grandpa was about to explain, but Mr. Delome waved him off and cast a meaningful glance at the lady as he dived into the story. "I was opening my curtains—I live across the street—and I saw these two children riding their bikes. The little boy turned back to look at his sister, and he crashed into the back side of the truck. He fell off the bike, and the girl screamed. Before I could hardly think, Mr. Moody had run out of the house. He talked to the little guy, walked with him to the driveway, and put his long-sleeved shirt on him."

Office Downing had been jotting notes on a clipboard, and Mitch thought he detected a hint of a smile. Joey's mom didn't say anything but her face portrayed she was upset. "Okay," the officer bent over and looked at Joey, "what do you think happened?"

Joey shrugged his shoulders. "That man told you already. Marcy was saying something to me, and I didn't watch where I was going. Then, I crashed, and Marcy screamed."

Marcy added, "If he'd been wearing his helmet, he wouldn't have that bump. I only screamed, Joey, 'cause I thought you were really hurt. We wanted to ride in the street even though we know we're not supposed to. I hope we didn't mess up the man's truck." She rubbed on the bumper. "I see a little scrape."

Officer Downing asked Joey's mom her name. "Marge Pair," she replied in an irritated tone. "I'd like to take Joey to the doctor."

Officer Downing nodded. "That's fine. Before you leave, I need your address."

After Mrs. Pair gave the information, Joey pulled Grandpa's shirt off. He smiled as he gave it back. "Thank you, Mister; it helped me get warm." Joey grinned as Mrs. Pair hurried the two children away.

Mr. Delome watched the officer continue to fill out the report. "I wonder who called you, although I know it was a wise idea since Mrs. Pair didn't seem too happy."

Officer Downing flipped through several papers on his clipboard. "We're not at liberty to share that, but it's unusual to come to an accident this minor." He shook Grandpa's hand. "If you'd like a copy of the report, I'll have it available Monday."

Grandpa and the children said good-bye to Mr. Delome and trooped in the house. Grandpa told the story to Grandma and Mom, who had watched from the window because they stayed with the twins. "That's too bad," Grandma seemed sad. "Maybe Joey will learn his lesson about not riding in the street and needing to wear a helmet."

"Hopefully. Joey and Marcy seemed to have sweet spirits, but Mrs. Pair was on the sour side. At least we'll have a report that documents the whole thing in case she comes back and says it's my fault."

Just before lunch, Dad called to see how the morning had gone. Mitch told him the story. "Dad, Grandpa didn't get angry. He listened to Mrs. Pair and was very calm . . . I'm afraid I would've been unhappy with her. Someone called the police. It was nice because the policeman was one of the guys who was at the bank's alarm."

That afternoon, the doorbell rang. Grandma glanced out the window. "It's not a delivery person—it's Mrs. Pair."

"I'll get it," Grandpa said firmly.

Grandpa swung open the front door and smiled. "Good afternoon, Mrs. Pair. How is your little boy?"

"You shouldn't have parked your truck in the street." Mrs. Pair ignored Grandpa's question, and her voice dripped of bitterness. "I expect you to pay every cent of my boy's doctor visit."

"So," Grandpa remained composed, "you're saying because I parked my truck next to the curb, I'm responsible for your son not watching where he was going, not wearing a helmet, and damaging my truck. My truck was legally parked on the side of the road. It wasn't in the middle where it would have been a hazard."

A sigh of frustration escaped Mrs. Pair's mouth, but she seemed to be calming down. Suddenly, her face changed, and tears filled her eyes. "I can't afford the doctor's visit because I was recently divorced, and I don't have any medical insurance."

Grandpa hesitated. "I'm sorry. You remind me of a similar situation every person is in."

"I don't understand what you mean."

Grandpa could tell he had Mrs. Pair's attention. "Each of us has a debt that we can't repay; it's impossible. Have you ever heard what Jesus did for you?"

"No, I'm not religious. Since my life has fallen apart, I've thought about trying it, but it seems hopeless."

Grandpa held the door open. "Why don't you come in?"

Mrs. Pair followed him into the living room and sat next to Grandma on the couch. Grandpa continued, "The first question I have for you is if you consider yourself to be a good person?"

Shrugging her shoulders, she said, "Yes. I'm not perfect, but then nobody is."

"Here's a quick test. Have you ever lied?"

"Maybe when I was a child."

"What does that make you?" Mrs. Pair paused. Grandpa waited and then prompted, "What would you call me if I lied to you?"

"A liar."

"Correct. Have you ever stolen anything?"

"Yes, I have, and that makes me a thief." Mrs. Pair was catching on.

"We won't go any farther then. By your own admission, you've said you're a lying thief. When you stand before God, and He judges you based on the ten commandments, would you say you're innocent or guilty?"

Mrs. Pair was quiet for a moment and then said, "I guess that means I'm guilty."

"Where would you go, to heaven or hell?"

"Hell."

"Does that make you concerned?"

"Yes."

Grandpa proceeded to share with her from the Bible how she could be saved. At the end, she seemed thoughtful. "I've never heard what you've told me before, so I'm going to have to consider this. I'm sorry I was angry with you. Thank you for taking the time to share with me."

"You're welcome." Grandpa pulled out his wallet and handed her several green bills. "This should help with your son's visit today."

Tears sprang into Mrs. Pair's eyes. "Thank you. I know I don't deserve it."

After Mrs. Pair left, a serious discussion followed with Grandpa and the children. They were amazed at his generosity to someone who wasn't gracious. He shook his head. "It's not about Grandpa, children. I was only obeying Jesus. He prompted me with the verse about loving my enemies and blessing them. Mrs. Pair is not my enemy, but let's say we could tell from the first interaction we had with her that she wasn't very happy with me. Giving her fifty dollars is a way I could bless her."

Chapter 14 | Best Resurrection Sunday

Two and a half weeks later it was April 10th, Resurrection Sunday. "Jesus is Risen!" Dad proclaimed, swinging open the boys' door and then the girls'. "What a wonderful Saviour! I just read the section in Matthew about His resurrection. Jesus paid the penalty for sin on the cross, but through His resurrection He conquered death."

Max sat up in bed. "May we bring the twins to church?"

Dad shook his head. "No. Mom and I prefer to keep babies home until they are six weeks old, because even a small cold is difficult on a baby and can lead to more serious complications."

"Okay," Max nodded. "Even though I'd really like to go to church, I'd be happy to stay with Mom."

"You may, Max. That'll give you, Mom, and the twins some special time together. I'm going downstairs to put the breakfast casserole in the oven."

At breakfast, discussion revolved around the rest of the day. "I wish Mr. Delome would come to church," Mitch remarked.

Dad took a bite before he responded. "I agree. The positive side is that he wanted to eat dinner with us, and he said he'd stay for devotions. Let's keep praying for his salvation."

After church and a light lunch (since the big dinner would be in the evening), the children had an idea. "Dad, may we take care of the twins so you and Mom can nap without having to worry about them?" Max wondered.

Dad smiled. "That would be good for Mom, and I'm feeling a bit weary myself. I assume you boys will watch Moses and Mollie will watch Melissa?"

"Yes, sir."

"I'll definitely enjoy a Sunday nap," Mom affirmed. "I'll go nurse the twins now."

"Dad," Mollie said, thinking ahead to dinner, "Mom told me that Max and I could make the potato casserole for the meal tonight. Is it okay if Mitch watches the twins on a blanket?"

"Yes. Remember Maple can't be in the living room if the twins are on the blanket."

"Yes, sir."

"Before church, Grandma and I discussed the meal. I told her we'll eat at six. She's bringing whole wheat rolls, baked beans, and dessert. Grandpa said they'll come early to help with preparations."

"What would you like us to do, besides the casserole?" Max wondered.

"Mom left a note on the counter with instructions. I skimmed it, and it said to preheat the oven and then put the ham in at a certain time. You can decide when you need to make the casserole. You can also set the table; Mom noted what dishes and tablecloth you should use."

The afternoon passed quickly, and Max, Mollie, and Mitch enjoyed their "job" of watching the twins. Finally, it was time to work on dinner. Mitch sat in the living room next to Melissa, who was lying on a blanket. "I'm hungry, Melissa. It'll still be a while before we can eat." Mitch continued to chat with Melissa, whose only response was an occasional grin.

Maddie thumped down the stairs from her nap, dragging her cuddle blanket. "I want to help Mollie." She rubbed her eyes.

"You may," Mollie agreed. "But, first, would you please go put your blanket upstairs? Dad and Mom want you to keep it in your bed."

"Okay," Maddie looked longingly at her special blanket. "I be back."

A minute later, Maddie was ready. "Let's set the table," Mollie decided. "Can you fold the napkins?"

"Sures I can."

Soon, the table was neatly set with Mom's special dishes and a white tablecloth and napkins. Around 4:30, Dad and Mom joined the children. Mom picked up Melissa. "How'd she do, Mitch?"

"Great! I've been watching her on the blanket since Mollie was working on dinner. Mollie said Melissa took a nice nap. Moses didn't nap earlier this afternoon, but he fell asleep on the blanket, so Mollie took him to the little crib."

Dad and Mom carried the twins upstairs so they could be fed. Dad hurried down to work with the children on more dinner preparations. A few minutes later, the doorbell rang, and the Moodys' grandparents stepped in. Grandpa carried several containers. "We made it!" he said, slightly out of breath. Maple bounded toward him, barking and wagging her tail. "Good pup, Maple; you don't need to bark. Christ is risen!"

"Hi, Grandpa and Grandma. I missed seeing you this morning; Mom and I had a nice time, though. What'd you make for dessert?" Max wanted to know.

Grandpa laughed. "Do you think I'm going to give away my secret? Should I tell, Martha?"

"Whatever you like, James."

Grandpa watched the four pleading faces. "Who can resist? The dessert choice—the only option I know how to make—is an Oreo ice cream dessert."

"That should be fantastic," Mitch declared.

"Hopefully. I didn't test it." Grandpa opened the freezer and stuck the dessert on a shelf. "Jim, I've wanted to get your opinion on something. I've been feeling a real burden about Mr. Delome's salvation. I'd like to talk to him privately about the whole plan of salvation. Maybe he has questions that I can help answer. I know he's heard most, if not all of it before, but I want to lay everything out plainly for him."

"I'd say go for it. Maybe he'll really listen. You're hearing the Holy Spirit speak to your heart. Joy will follow as you obey!" Dad hugged Grandpa, and the children watched quietly. Now they knew what they could pray about tonight.

An hour later, Mr. Delome arrived. "Good evening!" he greeted them. Everyone gathered at the table, and Grandpa blessed the food. Mr. Delome was happy to be included with the Moodys' festivities. "We never had get-togethers in my family," he mused. "But I like them."

At devotions, Mitch offered to share his Bible with Mr. Delome. Mr. Delome shook his head. "I'll listen."

Grandpa felt a pang of apprehension. Mr. Delome had always been willing to read along with someone. *Maybe he won't let me talk about Christ with him later,* Grandpa thought. Throughout devotions, Mr. Delome didn't say a word, and he had a faraway look.

Mitch silently prayed for Mr. Delome. *Please Jesus, help him want to accept You as his Lord and Saviour. Soften his heart. I know You're pleading with him. Help him to listen to Grandpa.*

After they finished reading in the Gospels about the Resurrection, they talked for several minutes. Mr. Delome seemed himself again, and Mom asked: "Would you like to hold Melissa?"

"I would, but she is so tiny. Do you think I would hurt her? I don't have much baby-holding experience," Mr. Delome said.

Dad encouraged Mr. Delome, "I believe you will do great. Maybe it has been a long time since you held a baby, but it is like riding a bicycle, you never forget. We will be right here if you are uncomfortable."

Mr. Delome reached out his arms, and Dad brought over the precious, small bundle. "She is real sweet," Mr. Delome remarked.

Nine o'clock came, and Mr. Delome handed Melissa to Dad. "I should head home. Thanks for the nice evening. Holidays can be lonely, and I was glad for something to do."

Grandpa stepped over next to Mr. Delome. "I'd love to walk home with you."

"Come right along. Good-bye everyone!"

Mitch shut the door behind them, paused, and then said in a loud whisper. "I wonder what Mr. Delome will say?"

Mr. Delome and Grandpa talked about the upcoming week as they walked across the street. When they reached Mr. Delome's front step, Grandpa motioned. "Could we sit here for a bit? I'd like to talk about something."

"Fine with me," Mr. Delome agreed. "I love this time of year: crisp, cool evenings, no bugs; it reminds me of the mountains. You know, I would move to Colorado if it weren't for the Moodys. They're almost like family to me."

The soft moonlight allowed Grandpa to clearly see Mr. Delome's face. "Well, Oliver," Grandpa paused. "I've had a burden on my heart; I'm very concerned about your soul and where you'll spend eternity. I know what it is like to live life without Jesus Christ—and there is no comparison to life with Him. I don't know if you've thought about eternity; it's never ending. I don't want you to spend eternity in hell."

Mr. Delome was silent, and Grandpa couldn't discern from his face what he was thinking. It didn't take long before Mr. Delome sighed. "James, I can't believe you're telling me this. I almost didn't stay for devotions tonight because I've been struggling. I'll tell you my background. I'm a member of a church, although you wouldn't know it from how often I go. I visit occasionally if I feel like it.

"I thought that being a church member and trying to be good was all a person needed to do to go to heaven. When I was over at Thanksgiving last year, and Jim shared Bible verses with you, and you prayed, I saw clearly that my church membership and being good weren't enough. I've considered what the Moodys have said, but the roadblock I can't get by is my past. I don't think God could or would want to save a person like me. I did too many bad things when I was younger."

Grandpa shivered. He wasn't sure if it was because of the coolness of the spring evening or from anticipation. He quickly prayed for wisdom before he responded. "You're right that church membership won't save you. Ephesians 2:8-9 says: 'For by grace are ye saved through faith; and that not of yourselves: *it is* the gift of God: Not of works, lest any man should boast.' Doing good things will not earn you that ticket to heaven. It's a gift through faith."

Mr. Delome shook his head. "But I don't have faith."

Grandpa pulled out his Soul Winner's New Testament. "Let me read verses to you that describe salvation. I know you heard these at Thanksgiving, but it's important that you listen very carefully. Romans 3:23: 'For all have sinned, and come short of the glory of God.' Oliver, we've all sinned. Every single person on this earth. Romans 6:23—wait, why don't you read it?" Grandpa handed his Bible to Mr. Delome. "Right here."

Mr. Delome slowly read, "For the wages of sin *is* death; but the gift of God *is* eternal life through Jesus Christ our Lord."

Grandpa nodded. "This means that the consequence for our sin, no matter how small, is death. Jesus Christ paid the penalty for our sin, if we'll receive Him and give Him our life. Now, Romans 10:9-11 next."

Mr. Delome continued, "That if thou shalt confess with thy mouth the Lord Jesus, and shalt believe in thine heart that God hath raised him from the dead, thou shalt be saved. For with the heart man believeth unto righteousness; and with the mouth confession is made unto salvation. For the scripture saith, Whosoever believeth on him shall not be ashamed."

"Good! You see, Oliver, that's where faith comes in. You mentioned your past. Here's what Paul says in 1 Timothy. 'This *is* a faithful saying, and worthy of all acceptation, that Christ Jesus came into the world to save sinners; of whom I am chief.'"

Tears trickled down Mr. Delome's cheeks. Grandpa laid his hand on Mr. Delome's shoulder. "I really care about where you'll spend eternity," Grandpa urged. He motioned to Mr. Delome's front window. "Remember when you had the fire last year? Did Jim walk over and knock softly on your front door, or did he bang on it and yell as loudly as he could for you to come out? If you hadn't answered the door, he would've found another way to alert you. That's the same way I feel about your soul. You are headed for a fire much worse than a house fire."

It appeared a battle was raging in Mr. Delome's soul as he tugged on a piece of grass and began tearing it into small pieces. Grandpa was not going to press for a decision, so he waited and prayed. Mr. Delome didn't wipe the tears off his face as he sniffled. "My heart has been so empty lately. I've seen something in the Moodys, though, that I long for— even in their children. They have a joy and a peace in their lives; their faith is evident to me. I want it for myself." Mr. Delome looked at Grandpa. "James, I'm ready—to give my life to Jesus. If He can save a person like the man you read about, He can save me. What do I do?"

Grandpa's heart leaped with happiness. "Pray. Tell Jesus what you have told me."

Mr. Delome and Grandpa kneeled on the rough cement. "God, I don't quite know what to say. I know I'm a sinner. I deserve hell. But, I ask for Your mercy. Lord, I believe You died on the cross for my sins and that God raised Jesus from the dead. I ask You to come into my heart and be my Saviour. I want to learn more about You. I pray that You would hear my prayer. In Jesus' Name, Amen."

Mr. Delome hugged Grandpa. "I'm saved! I know it!" he joyfully shouted.

Grandpa choked back his own tears. "Praise Jesus! That makes you my brother." Grandpa encouraged Mr. Delome to begin reading the Bible starting in the book of John each

Mr. Delome and Grandpa kneeled on the rough cement.

day and to tell others about Jesus saving him. After they talked for several minutes, Grandpa said good night to Mr. Delome and hurried across the street to share the news with the family. Grandpa knew the angels in heaven were rejoicing about another soul that had come home.

Chapter
15
Baking Project

Grandpa and Grandma continued to be a blessing to the Moodys by coming over each weekday. It was now Wednesday. "Oh no!" Grandma exclaimed to Mollie. "I forgot I have a doctor's appointment tomorrow."

"What for?" Mollie wondered.

"It's a follow up visit on my heart. I don't want not to be here tomorrow, but I can't reschedule the appointment."

Mom finished washing her hands in the kitchen sink and reassured Grandma. "Your help has been greatly appreciated, Mom; don't feel badly. We'll be fine tomorrow."

"Thank you, Emily."

Dad walked in from work. "Hello! I've missed everyone!" He kissed Mom and greeted the rest.

"We're just heading out," Grandpa explained. "By the way, Martha realized we forgot about her heart specialist's appointment tomorrow."

Dad stepped outside with them. "That's not a problem. I can't tell you how grateful I am for you and Mom coming over these past few weeks. I know you'll only be with us a week more before Emily takes back over. Grandma Clifton offered to help with anything following the twins' birth, and

I got the impression that she really wants to help in some way. I'll call her and see if she'd like to come over. If she's not able to, Emily will be fine."

"See you later!" Grandpa helped Grandma into the truck, and they drove off.

Mr. Delome saw Dad and hurried across the street. It was obvious he was a different person. His step carried a new spring, and he hummed a tune. "Good afternoon, well actually, evening!"

Dad smiled. "How are you today?"

"I'm blessed!" Mr. Delome grinned. "I got that term from you. I wondered if Mollie could throw together a pan of chocolate brownies for me tomorrow. I need them for a get-together with several old coworkers."

"She'd be happy to," Dad agreed. "Do you need them done by a certain time?"

"Anytime in the afternoon is fine. My get-together isn't until the next day. I really like white frosting on brownies; it seems to make a perfect brownie."

"She can definitely do that."

Mr. Delome added: "I'm looking forward to being with my old buddies. I can't wait to tell them about Jesus and what He's done in my life. James gave me his little Soul Winner's New Testament. Did you know he's going to do a Bible study with me once a week?"

Dad marveled at the sparkle he saw in Mr. Delome's face. "That's great news."

The next day, Grandma Clifton came over. "I left Honey at home because we don't need an extra dog," she said as Maple sniffed her. "You probably smell Honey." Grandma Clifton set a small tote bag next to the couch. "I brought my home-made tortillas for lunch."

"Thank you for coming," Mom was grateful.

"I wouldn't miss a chance to spend some time with the children and see the twins."

After morning school was done, the girls helped Grandma Clifton prepare lunch. Mollie heated refried beans to make burritos and told Grandma Clifton about her baking opportunity. "Mr. Delome asked me to do a pan of brownies. Mom said I can make them when my school is finished this afternoon."

"I know how much you enjoy baking, which is a good thing," Grandma Clifton encouraged. "Being able to cook and prepare meals is a way you can bless many, many people throughout your life."

The phone rang, and Max answered. "Hello . . . Yes, Mrs. Bagwell. How are you? . . . The twins are doing well. They don't sleep quite as much as they used to, so we can hold them more . . . Really? That is kind of you. Let me ask Mom, and I'll call you back."

Max hurried upstairs. "Mom, Mrs. Bagwell asked if she can bring dinner tonight . . . Okay, I'll tell her." Max came back downstairs and dialed Mrs. Bagwell's number. "Mrs. Bagwell, Mom said we'd love it . . . Thank you!"

After lunch, the children finished school for the day. Grandma Clifton read Maddie a book and then tucked her in for a nap. "Mollie, is there laundry I can fold?"

"Yes, ma'am. I washed and dried two loads this morning. You don't need to, Grandma Clifton. It's my job while Mom is recovering from the twins," Mollie explained.

"It'll give me something to do," Grandma Clifton insisted. Mollie and Mitch carried the baskets into the living room.

Mollie was ready to begin on her baking project. Max and Mitch wondered if they could help. "Yes," Mollie assured them. "Dad said we are to use two brownie mixes, and we'll need to make the frosting from scratch."

Max and Mitch whipped up the frosting while Mollie mixed the brownies. "Why does Mr. Delome want vanilla frosting on chocolate brownies?" Max asked. "We've only done chocolate before."

"Dad said he likes them that way," Mollie responded.

Mitch eyed the frosting. "Maybe we can try a brownie with the white frosting."

"We can! I'm making one big pan and a small one, that way the brownies are thicker than if we did two big pans."

While the brownies baked, Mollie organized the pantry, and the boys washed and dried dishes. When the brownies were done, Mollie placed the pans on the counter to cool, and then she went upstairs to wake Maddie from her nap. Maddie followed Mollie down to the kitchen. "I put out pretzels and juice for you," Mollie smiled encouragingly at her sleepy sister.

"Thanks, Mollie," Maddie munched on a pretzel. Mollie joined the rest in the living room. A minute later, Maddie ran into the room crying. Her fingers were covered in chocolate. "Ooooowwww!!" she sobbed, wringing her hand. "It HURTS!"

Mollie couldn't figure out what happened, until Max said, "She burned herself." He hurried Maddie to the kitchen sink, where he ran cold water on her hand, rinsing off the chocolate. He noticed two small blisters forming on her fingers. One glance at the smaller brownie pan told him she'd stuck her fingers in it.

Maddie was remorseful. "I'm really sorry, Max; I wanted to see what they looked like, and then I was going to ask Mollie if I could have one."

Max sensed her honesty and felt sympathetic. "I guess that was a hard lesson to learn. Remember Dad and Mom say never to touch anything on the counter unless they give you permission."

Maddie wiped tears from her eyes and brushed blonde curls from her face with her unburned hand. "I remember."

Grandma Clifton, Mollie, and Mitch gathered around Max and Maddie. "Are you okay?" Grandma Clifton wondered with concern.

Maddie shook her head. "No, I won't be until I ask Daddy's forgiveness for touching the pan. Do you have some of that jelly med-cine that you can put on my burn?"

Mitch went upstairs to find the desired gel. He brought it back, and Max decided they had run the cold water long enough. "We're going to spread some gel on the burn. It'll probably start to hurt since it's not under the water, but it shouldn't for very long after the gel starts working."

Maddie closed her eyes while Max applied the gooey, mint-smelling substance. "It still hurts!" she announced. "Can I look yet?"

"Yes."

"What are those bubbles?" Maddie seemed horrified. "I don't like them."

"They are blisters from the burn. In a few days, they'll go away."

Grandma Clifton decided she would occupy Maddie by working a few puzzles with her on the dining-room table. Max, Mollie, and Mitch finished cleaning the kitchen. "I think the brownies need to cool more before we frost them," Mollie decided.

"Okay," Max glanced at Mitch. "In the meantime, we should take Maple for a walk, so Mitch and I'll do that, right Mitch?"

"Sure, I'll find my shoes, and then I'll be ready."

When the boys had left, Mollie thought about what she could do to bless Dad and Mom. *The laundry is folded; that doesn't need to be done. I know! I can organize the coat closet.* Mollie worked diligently until she was through with the job. Grandma Clifton and Maddie had just finished a puzzle. "Would you like to help me frost the brownies, Maddie?"

"Yes, and I won't stick my fingers in it this time."

The girls frosted the brownies, and Mollie cut them into squares. They neatly arranged the brownies on plates. "We're going to take these over to Mr. Delome if it's fine with you, Grandma Clifton."

Grandma Clifton nodded. Maddie opened the closet door and said, "Mollie, you did a nice job."

"Praise Jesus. I wanted to bless Dad and Mom."

Mollie and Maddie put on their jackets. Maddie opened the front door for Mollie, who carried the two plates. "Good!" Mollie exclaimed. "There are the boys." Max and Mitch walked up the driveway with Maple. "Would you like to go with us to Mr. Delome's to deliver the brownies?"

"Yes. Let me take Maple inside first." Max stuck his head in the front door, and he unsnapped Maple's leash. "Grandma Clifton, Mitch and I are going with the girls. We'll be right back."

The four children walked across the street, with Mollie holding Maddie's hand. "Careful not to touch my burned fingers. May I ring the doorbell?"

"You may," Mollie said as they arrived at Mr. Delome's house.

Maddie rang the doorbell. The children heard footsteps, and Mr. Delome opened the door. "Here is my brownie delivery." He lifted the plastic wrap on one of the plates and popped a brownie into his mouth. "These are great!" Reaching into his pocket, he produced a five-dollar bill. "Thank you for the brownies, Mollie."

"You're welcome. I was happy to be able to do it."

"How are the twins?" Mr. Delome wondered.

"Good!" Max answered. "They're getting bigger. Grandma Clifton is helping today since Grandpa and Grandma had a doctor's appointment. Where are you reading in your Bible?"

Mr. Delome's face widened into a grin. "I've been reading John like your grandpa encouraged me. I go slowly, since I want to understand what I'm reading. I find myself picking up the Bible throughout the day to read! I love it."

"We're so glad, Mr. Delome." Mitch shook his hand. "We prayed for you for a long time."

"Thank you, Mitch. I thought I was a lost cause but Jesus reached down to save a sinner like me."

"We'd better be going home. Bye, Mr. Delome!" Max turned around and the other children followed.

On the way past the mail box, Mitch grabbed the mail and noticed the top piece. "We have a letter from our national pastor. I can't wait to read it!" The Moodys supported a native pastor in Africa and occasionally received a letter and a report from him on his ministry.

The children hurried into the house. They found Grandma Clifton and Mom in the living room with the twins. "Mom," Mitch started, "we received a letter from Pastor Kielebs. May I open it, and we children go outside to read it?"

"Yes."

Max, Mollie, Mitch, and Maddie took Maple outside and sat on the back porch, to read the letter. "Pastor Kielebs' daughter wrote you a letter." Mitch handed Mollie the eight-year-old's note.

Mollie's face sparkled as she read:

Dear Mollie Moody,

I liked your letter. It was nice. I accepted Jesus to be my Saviour when I was five. I don't have my own Bible, but I read my father's when he can spare it. I am trying to earn money from my little garden to pay for a Bible. I like to help my mother, and sometimes I'll visit grandmother. I pray for you every day. I love you.

Kelia

"I know what I'll do! Mr. Delome gave me five dollars. That should be enough to buy Kelia a Bible. I'll ask Dad to send the money in!" Mollie was excited.

"I know what I'll do . . .
That should be enough to buy Kelia a Bible."

The next morning, the family gathered around the table. Dad held Melissa, and Mom wore her new sling with Moses snuggled in it. "I like your sling, Mom," Mollie complimented.

"Are you going to get one too?" Mitch asked Dad.

Dad shook his head. "No. When the twins are old enough, I'll use our back-pack carrier for one of them."

Mitch spilt open a steaming, whole-wheat cinnamon muffin. "Moses and Melissa are growing fast!"

Mom agreed. "I realized this morning they are five weeks old. I've been very grateful for Grandpa and Grandma's help the last several weeks. Not only have they done school with you children, but Grandma has worked with Mollie on sewing, and Grandpa's been going through the plumbing book with the boys."

"It has been a blessing," Dad said. "Speaking of the twins, I'll stop by the baby store on my lunch break to purchase a crib divider. That will help us not need a new crib for a few more months."

"What's a crib divider?" Max wondered.

"It's a cushion that you can use to basically split a crib in half. Moses will have one section and Melissa the other. They're moving too much to be together. Miss Carolyn told Mom about this crib divider, and it'll save buying another crib for a little while. I've decided," Dad paused and could tell the children were eager to hear what he would say. "To call a Moody Family Fun Night. Can you all be ready tonight?"

"Yes, sir!" the children chorused.

"You may pick out what you want for dinner," Dad continued. "We'll do our family Bible time after that, and we'll also play Hide n' Seek."

"I'll stay in the bedroom with the twins," Mom offered, with a twinkle in her eyes.

"Sounds like a plan." Dad noticed Melissa was watching his fork. "Pretty soon she'll be too old to hold like this at mealtime. See her look at the fork? She'll start to grab for things next."

"Is today supposed to be a normal day?" Mitch asked Mom as he worked on breakfast cleanup.

"Yes. Friday morning chores and school. I also need the diaper pail emptied because it's quite full. It should be done every other day. Would you please try to remember?"

"Yes, ma'am."

A little while later, Grandpa and Grandma arrived. "Friday chores," Grandpa announced. "I didn't forget." He smiled at Mitch. "I think I'll work with you since you've been teaching me how to clean bathrooms. Which one shall we start with?"

"The one off the laundry room."

Mitch found the needed supplies, and Grandpa carried an armload of rags to the bathroom. "I've been practicing my cleaning skills at home," Grandpa confided to Mitch. "What do you want me to do?"

"What would you like to do, Grandpa?"

Grandpa surveyed the room. "I confess I like the mirror and sink best."

"Good." Mitch handed Grandpa two squirt bottles and several rags. Soon, they were chatting while they cleaned. "Nice job," Mitch commented as he surveyed the mirror.

"Really," Grandpa said as he vigorously squirted the sink, "tell me if you see anything wrong with my work."

"I think it looks good," Mitch encouraged. "I don't know how you manage not to have any streaks on the glass."

Mid-morning, the phone rang, and Grandma answered: "Hello . . . No, I'm the Grandma . . . Go ahead . . ." Grandpa and the children came into the room. Grandma mouthed, *"sales call."* She listened as the person continued to talk. Grandpa quickly grabbed a piece of paper and pencil and scratched a message. The note read: "Please witness—remember how I've done it?"

Grandma's face turned white, but she nodded at Grandpa. Max and Mitch began hopping around in excitement. Grandma was going to witness! Grandpa whispered that they should all be praying.

A few minutes later, Grandma said, "That sounds interesting. If my husband and I do go on a vacation, he likes to visit unusual places, probably not where one of your spots would be . . . Actually, there is. Since I've taken the time to listen to you, would you mind if I asked you a question? . . . Right, it's off topic. Is that okay? . . . Would you consider yourself to be a good person? . . . You would? Well, who wouldn't? Do you mind if I ask you several questions to see if that's true? They are simple and won't take long . . . The first would be have you ever stolen anything, even when you were a child? . . . Like a cookie? . . . I admit I have too. Then what does that make you? . . . Close; not a stealer, it starts with a 't'? . . . Thief, right! . . . Let's see," Grandma wiped her forehead. "Have you ever taken God's name in vain? . . . I used to do it all the time myself . . . God's Word says that is blasphemy. Have you ever wanted a thing that is not your own? . . . I have, too! That is called being covetous . . . By what we've talked about, you've admitted to being a thieving-blasphemous-coveter!

"Now, if God were to judge you by His ten command-ments—and we've talked about three of them—would you be guilty? . . . Yes, okay. Where would He send you? . . . To hell. Does that make you concerned? . . . Good; it should! . . . Do you know what God did for you? . . . He sent His only Son, Jesus Christ, to die on the cross for our sins . . . But, it involves repenting of your sin and believing Jesus died on the cross for your sins and rose again. Will you trust Him to be your Saviour? . . . Do you have a Bible? . . . I would encourage you to start in the book of John . . . Right . . . I was blessed to be able to talk to you, Michelle . . . I'll be praying for you. Good-bye."

Grandpa's face beamed as Grandma hung up. "You did it!"

"It was only because of your prayers," Grandma sighed. "The lady seemed open. She had a Bible, and she said she'd read in the book of John."

"Bless you, Martha. You don't know how Jesus will use that conversation in her life."

At lunch, since it was such a beautiful day, everyone ate out-side. Mom buckled the twins into the stroller Mr. Delome had given them. "Mitch, I remembered something when I was feeding the twins this morning."

"What's that?"

"You and Max have dentist appointments this afternoon."

Mitch's face fell, although Mom didn't notice. "Grandpa," Mom continued, "would you mind taking the boys? The appointments are at two."

"No problem at all, Emily."

At one-forty, Grandpa grabbed his keys from the counter. "We need to go. Love you, Martha," he gave her a quick kiss. "Do you have any other errands?"

"I don't. Can you children think of anything?"

"We need some cheese for dinner tonight. We're going to make the Italian stuffed bread, and we're out of mozzarella," Mollie said. "Dad told us we could buy two bags of chips. Could you pick out Dad and Mom's favorites?"

Grandpa nodded. "We'll drop by the grocery store on the way home. Bye!"

Chapter 16

Dentist Appointments

Mitch was unusually quiet as they drove down the road. Grandpa remarked, "I'll enjoy meeting the dentist. I've yet to find a dentist since we've moved. It's one of those things I've put off. I'm confident I'll like the dentist since your dad choose him for you." He glanced at Mitch. "What's bothering you?"

"I'm nervous about my appointment. What if I need a filling?"

Grandpa assured him, "Don't worry about that, my boy. You shouldn't have any problems."

There was a minute of silence until Mitch confessed, "I sometimes skip brushing my teeth at night if I'm too tired or don't feel like it."

"Oh, then that is serious, Mitch. You might see it as a little thing, but disobeying is not a small matter. You need to confess it to your parents tonight."

"Yes, sir, I will."

Grandpa shared with Max and Mitch about the importance of brushing their teeth. "My brother used to be a dentist. Of course, technology has really advanced over the years. He would always tell me these facts about plaque and how it grows." Max and Mitch found themselves unconsciously running their tongues over their teeth as Grandpa talked. "Well, here we are. I assume this is the right place."

"Yes." Max answered, and Mitch was quiet. They walked in, and a lady greeted them.

"Good afternoon. Please sign in," she tapped a clipboard. "We'll be right with you."

The waiting room was quiet; Grandpa pulled out his pocket New Testament and began reading to himself. Mitch sat stiffly in the chair, wishing he was at home preparing for their Family Fun Night. *Mollie's probably making the dough for dinner.* The door opened and banged shut. Mitch saw Mrs. Bagwell!

The receptionist smiled. "Good afternoon, Miss Bagwell."

"Hello," Mrs. Bagwell wrote her name and the time on the clipboard and continued, "I'm Mrs. Bagwell, not Miss. My husband died many years ago."

"Please accept my apologies, Mrs. Bagwell."

"Okay." Mrs. Bagwell turned and found a nearby chair.

"Hello, Mrs. Bagwell," Max greeted her.

Mrs. Bagwell seemed surprised. "I hadn't noticed you; you just brightened my day! What brings you here?"

"Mitch and I are going to get our teeth cleaned. What about you?"

"I need a crown. I didn't brush my teeth like I should have when I was younger, and now I'm paying the conse-quences—literally!"

Mitch's eyes widened. *Would this mean he would need a crown?* A lady stepped from behind a door. "Mitchell, we're ready for you," she motioned to Mitch.

"Could Max and I go back as well?" Grandpa asked.

"Right this way," she cheerfully invited, and they followed her. She found a stool for Grandpa, and Max offered to stand.

"My name is Amy, and I'll be cleaning your teeth. Following what I do, the doctor will be in to give the final check." Amy must have sensed Mitch's nervousness. "Have you been to a dentist before?" she sweetly asked.

"Yes, but I'm afraid I will need a filling."

Clipping a white bib around Mitch's neck, she reassured him. "Don't worry. Not many children have to have fillings, especially if you've been maintaining proper dental hygiene."

Mitch thought back to his health book and tried to remember what "hygiene" meant. *Hopefully it doesn't have to do with brushing teeth,* he thought. Amy's voice broke his concentration. "Here, please wear these glasses. They're to protect your eyes from this light." She handed Mitch a pair of large, dark glasses and tilted his chair back. Mitch tightly grasped the arm rests as Amy began cleaning his teeth.

Grandpa turned the conversation to spiritual things. He discovered that Amy was a strong believer. Finally, Amy patted Mitch. "You're almost through. I'll call the doctor for his exam."

Mitch breathed a sigh of relief. Obviously she hadn't found any cavities! Dr. Gray walked in and shook Mitch's hand. "Nice to see you again, buddy. How are you doing?"

"Pretty good," Mitch's voice squeaked.

"Great. Hello, Max, and may I guess, Grandpa?" Dr. Gray shook Grandpa's hand before pulling on a pair of white, stretchy gloves. "Mitchell, are you having any tooth difficulties?"

"No, sir."

"Open wide. Mmmmhhhhhhhhh." Mitch felt the poke, poke from the doctor's little tool on his teeth. "Right."

Max strained to watch the doctor. Dr. Gray seemed to be focusing on one tooth. *This might be bad news for Mitch,* he thought. Poke, poke, poke. Although the poking didn't hurt, Mitch wondered why the doctor kept working on the tooth.

"Open wide. Mmmmhhhhhhhhh." Mitch felt the poke, poke from the doctor's little tool on his teeth. "Right."

Dr. Gray turned to his assistant. "Please note on number twenty-eight, a small carie."

Mitch's heart sank. *Even though he didn't say cavity, it sounds like bad news.* "I'm afraid you do have a small cavity, Mitch. It's not a big deal, because it's one of your baby teeth. Since it's already loose, we're not going to fill it unless you're having pain. Are you brushing your teeth following every meal?"

Mitch knew he had to be honest. "Well, sir, I've sometimes skipped my evening brushing. I won't from now on!"

After Max's cleaning was completed, they drove to the grocery store. Mitch's heart was heavy, but he was looking forward to Dad coming home so he could confess his sin and ask forgiveness. That evening, Mitch raced to meet Dad. "I need to talk to you." Dad and Mitch went upstairs to the boys' bedroom. "I haven't always been brushing my teeth after dinner. Will you please forgive me for not obeying you and brushing my teeth when I should have? The dentist said I had a small cavity, but since it's in a loose baby tooth, I shouldn't have to get it filled."

Dad hugged Mitch. "Thank you for your tender heart. I will forgive you, Son. I trust you will obey now."

Dad and Mitch went hand-in-hand downstairs. "Is everyone ready for our Family Fun Night?" Dad asked.

Mom walked into the kitchen with Moses. "I am! Moses has been fussy since he woke from his nap. He doesn't seem happy being held or in his crib. Maybe if you took him for a while, he'll calm down. He seems to respond well to your voice!"

Dad snuggled the little guy. "What's the matter, Moses?"

"I'll bring Melissa down. Would you like to hold her?" Mom asked Max.

"Yes, ma'am."

Mom was soon back with Melissa. "Is there anything I can do to help with dinner? You children have done incredibly well with meals since I've had the twins. I've been very pleased with your initiative."

"I think we're about ready. The stuffed bread is done," Mollie said. "Dad let us buy two different kinds of chips. We got one bag of your favorite and the other of Dad's."

After dinner, the family gathered for time in God's Word. Mom laid the twins on a blanket. They cooed happily as Maddie shook a rattle from the activity gym. "I like the twins, Mommy. They are 'dorable babies. I really like holding them, but I can't do both of them at one time."

Mollie wiggled her finger near Moses. He reached out and clasped it with his tiny hand. "Moses, you precious man. You're happy now. It's funny, Mom. He's either really happy or really unhappy."

"Let's open our Bibles." Dad smiled at the girls. "I know we love those twins, but we need to put our attention on the Word, or we'll not have time for our evening plans."

"Yes, sir," both girls responded.

Halfway through devotion, Maple whined. "Quiet, Maple. Go lie down." When the twins were on the blanket, Maple was not allowed in the living room. With a grunt, she laid back down.

Maddie watched the situation. "Daddy," she urgently pulled on his arm. "I want to tell you something."

"What is it?"

"Maple's a real nice dog, but I think babies are much better than dogs. Babies are tiny, little people."

"I agree with you, Maddie."

The other children and Mom added their affirmation. "It's hard to imagine what life was like before the twins," Mollie sighed. "It's so normal now to see the two of them. I can't wait to watch them crawl. They'll be so cute."

When devotion was done, Dad and Mom carried the twins upstairs. Then Dad and the children played several rounds of Hide n' Seek. Maddie didn't want to be by herself in the dark, so she was Mollie's buddy. Max managed not to be found on any of the rounds, so Dad declared him the winner. Finally, the family gathered in the living room, and Mom came downstairs. "I tucked the twins in their crib. Did you have a good time?"

"We did," Mitch answered. "Max had the best hiding spot! We never found him."

Dad pulled Maddie onto his lap. "I believe a fitting way to close out our Family Fun Night would be to share something with you children. I can't tell you how blessed Mom and I've been over these last five and a half weeks since Moses and Melissa have been here. You children have pitched in and taken care of much of the household responsibilities. It's been hard, but you've willingly done it, knowing it was a blessing to Mom and me. You have showed maturity in many different areas. We're grateful to Jesus for the gift of children, and you all have truly honored and obeyed Mom and me, like Ephesians 6 talks about."

Chapter
17

Max's Birthday

Mitch woke up and heard Maple whine. "Not now, Maple," he murmured sleepily. Several minutes later, he realized the date: Saturday, April 23rd. *It's Max's twelfth birthday! I need to get up, because Mollie and I are supposed to decorate the house.* He slipped down the ladder and out of the room, with Maple following him. Quietly closing the door, he hoped Max stayed asleep. Dad and Mom were softly talking in their room. Maple heard Dad's voice and sat near the bedroom door. Mitch shook his head, whispering: "You can't stay there."

Mollie opened her door. "Good morning, Mitch. I'm having my devotions, and I'll be down later to help decorate. I'll bring the paper and markers to make Max's signs. Dad said we could tape the big one to the garage doors."

"Okay. Come on Maple; let's go outside."

At the word "outside," Maple trotted after Mitch. Even though she loved Dad, her next favorite thing was to be outside. Mitch let her out the back door and settled into Dad's recliner to have his time in God's Word. He flipped his Bible open to 2 Timothy chapter 3. He was near the end when he came to verse 16. "All scripture *is* given by inspiration of God, and is profitable for doctrine, for reproof, for correction, for instruction in righteousness." *Wow,* he thought, *God's Word is so powerful. I see how memorization is very good. One benefit of memorization is that Jesus brings verses back to my mind as I'm tempted or discouraged. Then, for the instruction in righteousness part, I'm learning how to live my life for Jesus through studying His Word. I can never read too much of the Bible. There's going to always be things to learn and understand!*

Mollie joined Mitch in the living room a half hour later. They worked hard on the garage-door sign, which read, "Happy 12th Birthday, Max! '. . . Blessed *is* the man *that* feareth the LORD . . .' Psalms 112:1."

Since it was Saturday, Dad was home from work. After a few minutes, Dad came down. Studying Mollie and Mitch's work, Dad complimented them. "I like the verse you used! Max is awake and having his Bible time. I asked him to stay in his room a little longer, because I knew you were decorating downstairs."

Dad helped the children tape their sign to the garage doors. Mitch attached several balloons to the sides. "I think that should work," Mitch decided. "What are we going to do today, Dad?"

"I don't have any plans, so we'll see what projects Mom would like to have done. There are always things to do around the house."

After breakfast, Mr. Delome stopped in. "I saw the sign and wanted to congratulate Max on his birthday. Is that the proper word?" he humbly asked Mom. "You're the expert schoolteacher."

Mom smiled. "Yes, it is."

Mr. Delome visited for a few minutes before pulling a piece of paper from his pocket. "I've been watching the vehicle ads; I found a van you might be interested in."

Max read the yellow-highlighted text out loud. "Family van, seats twelve. In almost-new condition, minor inside wear. Engine has been given regular maintenance. Call 913-555-6787; ask for Carl."

"Sounds like one we should check out," Dad agreed. "I'll take the birthday boy this afternoon if Carl is available."

Dad made a phone call, and Carl told him they were welcome to come look at the van. After lunch, Dad and Max left. "Do you think we'll get a new van today?" Max asked. "It would be a perfect birthday gift if we could all start going places together."

"I'd like to buy it, but we'll have to see what happens."

Twenty minutes later, they arrived at a three-story house. A man walked out, dressed in shorts and a t-shirt. "Hello! You must be Jim." He vigorously shook Dad's hand. "I'm Carl. Come on around back. I keep the cars out of sight."

"Do you have your own car dealership?" Max was surprised at the collection of ten vehicles.

Carl laughed. "It might seem like it; I do this as a side business. My wife doesn't like the cars to sit out front, so I park them in back. It's nice we live in the country, otherwise I'm sure our neighbors would complain."

Carl walked to a silver twelve-passenger van. "This is a great family van. I bought it from a friend up in Iowa. It had only been used occasionally at a Christian school and has about twenty thousand miles on it."

Dad examined the outside of the van and asked if he could test drive it. "By all means!" Carl handed Dad the keys.

On the drive, Max could tell Dad liked the van. "It seems like we're much higher up than we are in our van," Max commented.

"It is a taller ride," Dad agreed.

When they arrived back at Carl's house, Dad asked Carl several questions about the van. Finally, Dad said, "I know you're asking more, but I can offer you ten thousand. I have seven in a savings account, and the other three I could get by selling my current van."

Carl stuffed his hands in his pockets. "I don't know; I've just started advertising it." He thought for a few moments, and Max eagerly waited, confident this would be the answer to their prayers.

Shaking his head, Carl said, "I can't for ten. How about thirteen? I would give you a small loan for the difference."

"I'm sorry, Carl. I don't feel the Lord wants me to go into debt for this. What He wants me to have, He will provide

"This is a great family van . . ."

the finances for without having to borrow. I really appreciate being able to look at it."

"Let me know if you change your mind."

In the car, Max uncharacteristically felt like crying. "Dad!" he wailed. "We didn't get the van! What are we going to do?"

"Max, like Mom and I have discussed, there's no need to worry. If Jesus gave us the twins, which He did, He can provide for a van if we really need one."

"I know you're right; I'm just disappointed. Thank you for reminding me." Max smiled and determined to be cheerful.

Dad's cell phone rang. "Hello? . . Sure, here he is . . ." Dad handed the phone to Max. "It's Grandpa."

"Hi, Grandpa! . . . Thank you . . . Yes, sir. Dad and I looked at a van . . . No, we didn't, because the price was too much . . . We'll miss you tonight . . . Please tell Grandma I hope she feels better soon . . . I love you too. Good-bye."

"It sounds like Grandma has a small case of the stomach flu. Grandpa said he was sorry to miss my birthday evening, but he's going to stay home to take care of her."

That night, after dinner, family devotions, and Max's birthday party, there was still time for a walk. "Let's use the new stroller for the twins," Dad suggested.

It was a beautiful spring twilight—around sixty degrees. Dad buckled the twins securely into the double stroller. "Would the birthday boy like to push it?"

"Yes, sir!"

"May I ride my bike?" Maddie wondered.

"Me, too?" Mitch asked.

"Go ahead."

Just then, a horn beeped, and a vehicle slowed down. A man with a ball cap and bib overalls on rolled down his window. "Howdy, Moodys!"

"Sunflower Animal Control" was on the side of the truck. "Mr. Gibson!" Dad exclaimed. "Why it's been a long time since we've seen you! How've you been?"

"Jis fine. I got wind that yer wife had two babes. Congrats! My coworker who lives over here told me about it. I've been waitin' fer a chance to tell you how great that is."

"Thank you; we're very blessed. How is work going?"

"Fair. I'm looking at retirin' soon, if I can possibly squeeze by. I've been waitin' fer a creature to catch at yore place."

Dad laughed. "We've had enough excitement without that."

"I'm sure that's true. Well, I'd best be gittin' on my way. Nice to see you folks."

"God bless you," Dad said.

Several houses up, the Russells were outside, working in their yard. Madison, their baby, was in a stroller. "Hello!" Mr. Russell called.

He strode toward them, and Mom walked over to Mrs. Russell. "I haven't seen you for a long time!" Mom commented.

"I know. We've both been busy with our babies. I went back to work two weeks ago, and between that and taking care of Madison, life has been crazy." Mrs. Russell brushed back her hair.

"Life does stay busy," Mom agreed.

"I've wanted to talk to you about something that I've been thinking about quite often," Mrs. Russell paused. "I'm concerned about Madison's future. I thought I found a good daycare, but I'm not pleased with it. On the other hand, I don't want to give up my job just to raise Madison. Our income would be cut in half, and besides, the thought of being home all day is unbearable."

Mom nodded. "Years ago, I wouldn't have imagined myself having six children, being at home, and homeschooling them. However, you are the only one who can raise your child—there are many others who can fill your for-pay job. The question is—is your child worth it? I can tell you from my perspective that he is."

Setting down her shovel, Mrs. Russell looked at Madison, who was sound asleep. "I think that is the truth I have come to see but didn't want to accept. I expected you to say what you said. I needed some encouragement to help me to do what is right but also what I fear. I wonder if I could work from home, though," Mrs. Russell sounded hopeful.

"The problem is your attention would still be divided between work and family. What does Dave think of you staying home?"

Mrs. Russell's cheeks turned a light pink. "He likes the idea. He's been pushing for me to do it."

Mom smiled. "You'll never regret staying home. I'll be praying for you!" They talked a few minutes longer before Dad was ready to continue.

Chapter 18

Homeschool in Real Life

Grandpa and Grandma were finished helping at Moodys after almost five weeks. Mom was now easing back into "normal" life. "Good morning," Mom greeted Max as she grabbed a loaf of bread from the freezer. "Would you mind getting Moses? It sounds like he woke up. I'm hoping Melissa sleeps a little longer."

"Yes, ma'am."

After breakfast, Dad left for work, and Mom showed the children the new school schedule. "Since I'll be in and out with nursing the twins, I rearranged the schedule from when Grandpa and Grandma were here."

"I like to help Maddie," Mollie smiled. "It makes me feel like you!"

Mid-morning, Max worked on a science lesson while he sat near Moses and Melissa, who were laying on a blanket in the living room. Melissa giggled, reaching for a toy that dangled over her from the small play center Grandpa and Grandma had given them. Moses let out a happy laugh. Max sighed. *Molecules are way too confusing. I'll be at this all day, and I still won't get it.* He scratched his head in frustration and closed the book.

Mom walked in. "How's your work going, Max?"

"Terrible. I'll never be able to understand molecules. I don't think I need to learn science, anyway."

Mom's heart sank. *Why did Max have a bad attitude on her first day without help? Not to mention Maple wasn't obeying, and Maddie complained of a sore throat. If I call Jim, he'll talk to Max, and then I won't have to worry about it.* Mom felt immediate conviction from the Holy Spirit. *Yes, Lord, my attitude is wrong,* she silently prayed. *Please forgive me. Help me to be patient with Max.*

Mom put a smile on her face, even though she didn't feel like it. "Let's see if we can work through this together."

Max sighed and flipped the book open. "I read the section, and I still can't figure it out. Can I just skip the questions and move on to the next section?"

Mom shook her head. "No, we're going to persevere and learn it."

Mom spent the next half hour patiently working with Max. She could tell his heart was softening. At last, Max hugged Mom. "Please forgive me for my bad attitude. I'm very grateful for your help."

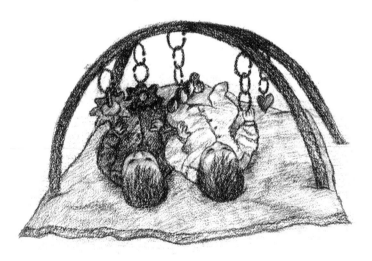

Melissa giggled, reaching for a toy that dangled over her . . .

Max finally understood the concept after his attitude changed, and the rest of the school day passed smoothly.

That evening at dinner, Mitch brought up the need for a bigger van. "It was hard yesterday not being able to go to church together!" he mourned.

Dad shook his head. "Like I've said before, since Jesus gave us the twins, He'll provide for our true needs. Obviously, since we have two vehicles, we don't really need the bigger van. Emily, I don't know what brought this to mind, but our anniversary is fast approaching. Do you have any ideas for how you'd like to celebrate?"

Mom shook her head. "Dinner out would be hard with the twins."

Max glanced at Mollie and Mitch and then back at Dad and Mom. "We've been discussing an idea," Max said. "Would you mind if I told you?"

"Go ahead, Max."

"We thought we could make a really special dinner for you. It'd be like your own little restaurant here at home. Grandma even said she would watch the twins that evening."

Dad saw the pleasure in Mom's eyes. "I like your idea!" Dad agreed. "I'll give you money to buy whatever you need for the meal. Maybe Grandpa can take you grocery shopping."

Mom smiled. "I think we'll enjoy a special anniversary dinner and time together."

One evening the next week, the Moodys were near the end of their Bible time when Grandpa and Grandma popped in. "Come, join us," Dad invited.

"Thank you! We've been working in the garden," Grandpa announced.

Grandma laid her hand on Grandpa's arm. "This man has truly changed. Grandpa had always said it was my job to work in the garden, and he didn't want to work with me. Since last Thanksgiving, when he accepted Jesus as his Lord and Saviour, things have been different. He's wanted to spend time with me. Today, he joined me in the garden! You should have seen how well he tilled the garden," Grandma complimented.

Grandpa grinned. Then, he suddenly apologized, "I'm sorry; here we are talking, and you're not through with God's Word."

"That's fine," Dad responded. "We had just finished reading. Does anyone have offenses to deal with?"

"I do," Max said. "I was angry with you, Mollie, when you asked to hold Moses because I wanted to as well. Please forgive me."

"I forgive you."

The Moodys sang "Down at the Cross." Mom offered Melissa to Grandpa and Moses to Grandma. "We did have a reason to stop over," Grandpa said. "Of course, it's nice to see you, but I thought it'd be easier to talk in person than on the phone."

"You have me curious now." Dad gave a warning look to Maple who was trying to inch closer to Grandpa. "No, Maple. Go lie down."

"I know your hearts are burdened for the neighbors' salvation. We're thrilled about Mr. Delome's salvation, yet there are so many others. Martha and I are feeling a real passion for lost souls, although since we live in the country, we have hardly any neighbors." Grandpa paused and tickled Melissa. She giggled. "What would you think of a once-a-month prayer time dedicated to our neighbors' salvation?"

"Yes!" Dad immediately agreed. "We could do it the first Friday evening of each month, starting tomorrow. Let's invite Mr. Delome, too."

The phone rang, and Max hurried to answer it. "Someone for you, Dad," he announced. Dad left the room, and the family talked while he was gone.

Dad came back with a large smile on his face. "That was Carl."

"What did he want?" Max seemed to know who this person was and could hardly contain his excitement.

"Carl, the man who owns the van we looked at on Max's birthday, said ever since we stopped by, I've been on his mind. I guess he'd written my phone number down on his desk calendar. The van we looked at isn't selling. It was odd, he thought, because it was a good price. He said he feels like he should sell it to me for ten thousand. He told me he hasn't been able to sleep the last few nights, thinking about it. He asked if I'd like it, and if so, I could come and take care of the details. He'll even take our current van as a trade-in. Wow, thank You, Jesus!"

"DAD!!!" Max, Mollie, Mitch, and Maddie gave Dad a group hug.

"Praise Jesus!" Max shouted. "We're going to have a new van!"

"When can we get it?" Mitch wondered.

"Tomorrow evening. We'll do it before prayer time. I'll leave for work early so we can begin our evening sooner," Dad decided. Lively talk continued about the van, until Grandpa said he and Grandma needed to go home.

The next morning, Maddie climbed on a step stool, looking at the calendar. She was learning the days of the week. "Friday. Is it the sixth?"

Max glanced over. "Yes, it is. You're learning to recognize your numbers."

Maddie wore her favorite red jumper, but her curls were a tangled mess. She brushed them back and traced the letters on the calendar. "This is an 'M.' What's the whole word, Max? I don't think it's Maddie."

"No, it's May. Remember: January, February, March, April, *May.*"

"Oh, yes."

Mom walked into the room with Melissa in her arms. "Good morning, Maddie." She kissed her and then laughed. "Your jumper is getting too short! You must be growing. And your hair! It doesn't look like Mollie helped you."

"No, she didn't. She was too busy, and I didn't want to wait. I've been looking at the numbers on the calendar, like you told me. Mommy, I like my favorite jumper. I don't want it to be too short. Can you fix it?"

"I doubt it. I've lengthened it as much as I could. We even put an extra section of fabric on the bottom of it last year. Let's make you a new red jumper."

"Mom, I'll hold Melissa," Max offered.

"Thank you. Maddie, we'll go upstairs to brush your hair."

The morning and afternoon passed quickly. Dinner was eaten at 4:30, with family devotions following. Dad decided to take Max and Mollie to trade in the old van and purchase the new one. An hour later, the silver van pulled into the driveway. Mitch and Maddie jumped around on the front step in eager anticipation.

"We have time for a quick ride," Dad decided. He hurried into the house to get Mom, the twins, and their car seats. Max carried Maddie's booster seat.

As Dad and Mom buckled in the car seats, the children explored the van. "Look at the smooth long seat," Maddie exclaimed, running her hand over the bench seat.

"The windows are so clear," Mollie admired.

After everyone had their seat belts on, Dad started the van. "It would be fitting to pray and ask the Lord to bless this van. Dear Heavenly Father, thank You for Your gift. Please protect us every mile that we drive. Please help us to use it in only ways that You would want it used. Thank You for moving in Carl's heart to allow us to purchase it. All praise and honor and glory to Your Name, Amen."

The family enjoyed their fifteen-minute ride. They pulled into the driveway at 7:35, and the prayer time was scheduled to begin at 7:45. Everyone was ready when the doorbell rang. "Good evening," Dad shook Mr. Delome's hand. "We're thrilled you're joining us!"

"I wouldn't miss it, Jim!"

Grandpa and Grandma stepped in behind Mr. Delome. Maple ran toward Grandpa barking. Melissa began crying, and Mom told Dad, "I'm going to rock her, feed her, and put her to bed. Would you mind bringing Moses upstairs for me? I'll feed him too and then put him to sleep."

"You can sit on the couch, if you'd like," Mitch offered to Mr. Delome.

"What if I prefer to kneel?" Mr. Delome shocked Mitch with his question.

"That's certainly fine," Mitch stuttered.

Grandpa smiled, hearing the interaction. *Mr. Delome's a new man,* he thought.

"I saw the van outside! Did you just buy it?" Mr. Delome wondered.

"Yes, tonight! Remember how you showed us the 'van for sale' ad on my birthday?" Max asked. "We went to look at it, but the man wouldn't take the price Dad could offer. Then, the man called Dad last night and said we could buy it for the lower price!"

"Wow!" Mr. Delome nodded. "I will have to write that down, as I'm trying to keep track of answered prayers so that I can see how the Lord works."

"I think we're ready," Dad decided. "Our time won't be limited to just our neighbors' salvation; you may pray about anything else you think of. We'll go ahead and start without Mom; she'll be down after settling the twins for bed."

The next hour and a half was a glorious time of the Moodys, Grandpa, Grandma, and Mr. Delome pouring out their hearts to Jesus. One of Mr. Delome's prayers touched everyone. "Dear Heavenly Father, please help me know how I should pray. I'm learning, and I'm eternally grateful for this family who shared Jesus with me. They could have stayed to themselves and hoped I'd someday hear. They made me feel loved and welcome in their family; I know they prayed for me, and they shared Jesus with me. I thank You for the burden You put on James' heart to be very bold with me, even if I didn't act like I wanted to hear it. Lord, I pray for the souls outside this house. Souls that are lost and dying and going to hell. Help us to share Jesus with them. I pray You'd help me not be timid. I want to be bold for You. Amen."

Chapter 19

An Anniversary to Remember

Plans were under way for the special anniversary dinner on May 13th. Thursday, the 12th, promised to be a busy day. After school was finished, Grandpa dropped by to take the children shopping. "Hello! Anyone home?" Grandpa lowered his voice, in sudden remembrance that the twins were likely sleeping.

"Hi, Grandpa," Maddie's muffled words came from the closet. Grandpa opened the closet doors.

"What are you doing in there?"

"I'm trying to find my shoe. Then, I heard someone coming, so I closed the doors because I didn't know who it was. Grandpa, I think Maple took one of my shoes, because I can't find it. Will you wait for me? I want to go; Mommy said I could if I tooked my nap, and I did already take it."

"We can wait for you. Maybe we'll have to buy you a new pair of shoes," Grandpa suggested.

"That'd be too much money," Maddie shook her head importantly. "Can you help me find it? I already checked the shoe chest, but it wasn't there. I thought maybe I put it back here. It looks like this." She thrust a pink and white sandal toward Grandpa.

Maple trotted in, and Grandpa let her sniff the sandal. "Go find it Maple." She cocked her head, and then left the room.

A minute later, she bumped Grandpa's leg with the lost sandal. "Good girl, Maple!" Grandpa praised her.

"How did you do that?" Maddie wondered.

Grandpa laughed. "I don't know! I thought it would be worth a try, and I guess she's a pretty smart dog. Are the dog biscuits still in the pantry?" Grandpa asked Max, who walked into the room.

"Yes, they are."

Grandpa found the desired item and gave it to Maple, who promptly gobbled it up. "Are you children ready to go? Grandma had laundry to do, so she stayed home."

Mollie and Mitch joined them. "We're ready," Mitch said. "Dad gave us money, and Max has the grocery list."

As they pulled out of the driveway, Grandpa noticed the house for sale next to the Moodys. "They must've just put the sign up," he remarked.

"Yes—yesterday. Dad talked to the man this morning. He indicated his job is moving him out to the East Coast," Mitch informed. "He's certainly not open to spiritual things. Dad's tried."

On the way to the store, the children told Grandpa the meal plans. "We were going to make a menu with several different options. We decided it'd be too hard to prepare a few main dishes, so we're going to design a menu that only has one option for each course. We want to do a menu so it feels more like a restaurant."

"Did you know I used to work at a restaurant?"

Max was amazed. "Grandpa, I think you've done almost every job there is."

"Not quite, Max. I'll give you 'waitering' tips at dinner tonight."

"Dinner?" Mitch wondered.

"We asked your parents if we could have you for dinner after we shopped. I said I'd take you back in time for family devotions."

"I can't wait!" Mollie's face shone with anticipation.

Grandpa pulled into the grocery store's parking lot. "Grandma wanted me to buy a few vegetables while we're here. The doctor was pleased with her last appointment; he said to keep eating those vegetables!"

While the children chose the brand of lasagna noodles they should get, Grandpa turned to a young man who was stocking the shelves. "Have you worked here long?"

"Only a year."

"Do you get Sundays off?"

The young man shook his head. "No, but I don't care. Sunday is the same as any other day."

Grandpa pulled a tract from his pocket. "Are you interested in spiritual things?"

Pretending not to notice the tract, the young man rearranged several items. "Not at all."

"Do you ever think about where you'll spend eternity?"

"No." The young man's face turned into a scowl, and Grandpa could tell he was not open.

"Here, even if you don't want to think about it, this is something for you to read."

"I don't want it."

Grandpa's heart was heavy as he joined the children. They turned down another aisle, and Grandpa sighed. "It's not easy when someone rejects the gospel."

"I know, Grandpa, but keep trying," Mitch encouraged.

Back at Grandpa and Grandma's house, Mollie placed the cold items in Grandma's refrigerator. "We'll have to remember to get your groceries out of the fridge when you go home," Grandma said. She flipped a grilled cheese sandwich over.

"Oh yummy!" Mollie exclaimed. "You're making grilled cheese!"

Grandma found a platter from the cupboard as she responded. "I thought I recalled you children liked grilled cheese sandwiches."

"We do, and Max especially does."

After Grandpa blessed the food, Mitch was eager to learn Grandpa's restaurant tips. "Would you please tell us now?"

"Yes. Let me think." He popped a grape into his mouth and crunched it. "Good grapes, Martha. We'll have to get more of them. All right, the number-one thing is the customer's first impression. That means you must have a professional dress code."

Maddie carefully broke off a section of grapes before asking: "What's that mean?"

"You don't want to look sloppy. For guys, it means you need to wear nice pants, shirt, and a tie."

"Oh." Maddie picked a grape from her bunch and observed it closely before eating it.

"So," Grandpa continued, "we wore white shirts with black pants. The ladies wore white blouses with black skirts. Jumpers should work fine, though. We guys also had little bow ties we clipped right here." Grandpa pointed to his neck.

"Do you have a black or navy blue jumper?" Grandma asked Mollie.

"Yes, ma'am."

"Besides how you dressed," Mitch was getting excited, "please give us tips on how to serve people."

"One of the marks of a good waiter was to be able to remember people's orders, without needing to write it down. Plus, it was important to deliver the meal correctly and not have any complaints from the customers. I always kept their glasses full. It was unacceptable to have them ask for a refill because I hadn't been watching. The fancy restaurants use cloth napkins and tablecloths. Grandma, do you have some the children could borrow?"

"I do; I've been thinking about what I should outfit them with."

After dinner, the children helped Grandpa clean up while Grandma found items for the special event. At 6:30, Grandpa took the children home. They even remembered to grab the cold groceries for the anniversary meal from Grandma's refrigerator.

The next afternoon, Mom promised to stay out of the kitchen and dining room as the children prepared the anniversary meal. Max and Mitch began the lasagna while

Mollie started reading the recipe card for their special dessert, This-n-That. It was a dessert Mom had grown up enjoying.

This-n-That

First Layer

1½ packages graham crackers, crushed
1 stick of butter, melted

Crush graham crackers with a rolling pin until they become thick crumbs. Melt the butter. Mix the cracker crumbs and butter together, then spread evenly in the bottom of a 9x13 pan. Set the pan in the freezer to harden while the next layer is being mixed.

Second Layer

1 cup powdered sugar
1 cup Cool Whip (purchase large container of Cool Whip; use the extra as the topping)
8 ounce package cream cheese

Soften cream cheese. Mix cream cheese, Cool Whip, and powdered sugar together until smooth. Take crust out of freezer and spread Cool Whip mixture evenly on the crust. Set in the refrigerator.

Third Layer

2 small packages butterscotch instant pudding
3¾ cups cold milk

Pour pudding mix into a bowl and add milk. Beat until thoroughly mixed. Pour mixture onto the next layer. Put the pan back into the refrigerator until the pudding is firm, about a half hour.

Add the extra Cool Whip as the topping. Place in refrigerator.

"Won't Mom be surprised when she's served this for dessert?" Mollie crushed the graham crackers with a rolling pin. "We haven't had it for over a year."

"Are we making this fancy enough?" Mitch eyed the lasagna noodles boiling in the pot.

"Yes. Grandpa told us a dinner of salad, lasagna, and garlic bread could easily be fifteen dollars each at a restaurant. He said dessert is usually expensive. This-n-That looks pretty fancy," Max assured Mitch.

Maddie had been coloring the cardboard bow ties. She slid off her chair, holding one up. "See? Is it good?"

Max examined it closely. "I think so. Great work, Maddie! Why don't you find your apron and see about helping Mollie?"

"Okay. May I wear the new one from Grandma?"

"Not yet; it's your special one for tonight. Here, I'll let you mix up the crust," Mollie smiled at Maddie.

By four, the dessert was finished and chilling in the refrigerator. Max and Mitch continued to work on the lasagna. Dad called and told the children he'd be home soon. He asked if he should come in the front door to avoid seeing anything. "Yes, that would probably be good," Max said. "Although you'll be able to smell what we're preparing!" Six was the time set for the big dinner.

Max slid the lasagna into the oven at five. "We need to get the kitchen cleaned up!" Mitch remarked as he began washing dishes.

"May I go upstairs to Dad and Mom?" Maddie requested.

"Yes," Max approved, "but please don't tell any secrets."

"I won't!" Maddie bounced out of the kitchen and knocked on Dad and Mom's door. "It's me, Maddie. I want to come in!"

Dad and Mom were sitting on the bed talking. "I came to take a break," Maddie snuggled next to Dad. "We've been workin' on dinner. Are you excited?"

"I'd say we are." Dad tickled Moses. "Can you smile? Ah, there it is." Dad made a funny face.

"I need to go now." Maddie jumped off the bed and ran out. Not seeing the boys upstairs, she went to the kitchen.

Just then, a knock was heard. "I know we didn't invite Mr. Delome," Mitch stated. "Grandma wasn't coming until closer to 6."

"We're early," Grandma announced as she and Grandpa stepped in. "Grandpa wanted to drop me off and see the preparations. He's going out for dinner with Mr. Delome tonight."

"We'll show you our setup," Max offered. Grandpa and Grandma walked around and complimented the children on the way everything was done.

"It was because of your help that it looks this way," Mollie acknowledged.

Grandma hurried upstairs a few minutes before six so she could receive instructions on the twins' care. Exactly at six, Dad and Mom walked downstairs. A sign at the bottom of the stairs read, "Please take a seat on the couch." Dad's eyes twinkled at Mom as they followed the directions.

Max and Mitch appeared a minute later. A white towel was laid over Max's arm, which Dad and Mom both noticed, a sure sign of a fancy restaurant. "Good evening, sir," Max addressed Dad. "How many tonight?"

"Two, and please make that non-smoking," Dad couldn't resist adding.

Mitch barely suppressed a laugh. "Come right this way," Max motioned to Dad and Mom.

Mom's eyes sparkled as she saw the table: a pearl-white tablecloth, silver-etched dishes, cloth napkins, and a centerpiece made of three candles, white lights, and greenery. Dad pulled Mom's chair out for her.

A white towel was laid over Max's arm, which Dad and Mom both noticed, a sure sign of a fancy restaurant.

"We'll be right with you for drink orders," Mitch handed Dad and Mom a menu and slid into the kitchen between make-shift curtains the children had rigged so that the kitchen activity couldn't be seen.

"Wow!" Mitch exclaimed in a loud whisper to Mollie. "Dad and Mom are all dressed up—Dad's wearing a suit!"

Mollie and Maddie emerged from the kitchen. "What may I get you to drink?" Mollie questioned.

Dad noticed Mollie didn't have a notepad. "Go ahead, Dear," he said to Mom.

Mom scanned over the neatly printed drink titles. "I'll take lemonade please."

"And for you, sir?"

"Lemonade would be great."

"Very good. We'll be back with your drinks."

Soon, Maddie brought one glass and placed it in front of Mom. "There you go, Mommy."

Before Maddie said anything more, Dad saw a small opening in the navy curtains, and a voice was heard. "Ma'am, Maddie!"

"Ooops," Maddie gasped. "I mean, ma'am."

"What a cute apron she had on!" Mom remarked after Maddie left. "I have a feeling Grandma let her borrow it."

Maddie was soon back with the other glass. "There you go, sir. Someone will take your order in a minute."

Dad noticed the children had set up the kitchen CD player in the corner, and soft music filled the room. Dad and Mom talked quietly. Mom sighed. "Jim, we have been blessed so much over these last 13 years of marriage. I'm very grateful for what the Lord Jesus has done in our lives—we've changed a lot since we made that commitment to each other."

Dad nodded. "You're right. I can't tell you what a blessing you are to me, Emily. Do you remember the day I came to you and said I felt we should homeschool the children? I know you weren't very excited about it, but you never complained."

Just then, Max carried in two salads. "These are complimentary with your meal. What dressing would you care for?"

"French, please, for both of us."

"Very well."

Mitch delivered the salad dressing. "What can I get for you tonight?"

Mom said, "I'll take the Classic Lasagna with the Crunch Garlic Bread."

"I think I'll have the same thing."

After Dad and Mom were served their main course, the plan for the rest of the dinner was being discussed in the kitchen. Max spoke: "Mollie and Maddie can go ahead and eat, and Mitch and I will keep an eye on Dad and Mom. We'll eat after you're through."

Mitch kept Dad and Mom's drinks filled to the brim. When the lasagna and garlic bread were eaten, Max cleared their plates. A few minutes later, Mollie asked, "Would you like dessert tonight?"

"Sure," Dad agreed.

"I'm sorry that wasn't on the menu," Mollie apologized. "I'll bring your dessert right out."

Mollie and Maddie carried generous-sized pieces of This-n-That to Dad and Mom.

"Thank you," Dad said.

Mom took several bites and smiled. "I can't believe how wonderful the dessert is! This is the first time the children have made it. I must admit, Jim, at first I felt a little disappointed we wouldn't be going out for our special date. But, I also knew it would be hard in terms of timing to leave the twins. This has been our best anniversary date yet! The food was delicious, our fellowship even more so, but what meant the most to me was the children's effort and love."

Dad squeezed Mom's hand across the table. "I totally agree. Emily. I also want you to know you are an incredible wife. You've stayed home for so many weeks because of the twins, and you haven't been unhappy."

They lingered at the table, reminiscing over the last few years. When they were done, they walked into the kitchen. Dad and Mom hugged each child. Mom had tears running down her face. "Thank you so much. Dad and I decided this has been our best anniversary. I can't tell you how much we've enjoyed it!"

"It was a very special evening, children," Dad beamed. Max, Mollie, Mitch, and Maddie's faces glowed with pleasure.

"We're glad; Jesus gave us the idea," Max said.

"I'm sorry I called you Mommy, 'cause I was only supposed to call you 'ma'am.' But, I can call you Mommy again," Maddie hugged Mom.

Chapter 20 | Nursing Home

One evening, Dad suggested they go visit the nursing home on Saturday. "They'd love to see the twins."

"I think that's a wonderful idea, Jim, although you always have great ideas! Could we bring Grandma Clifton along? We haven't been with her much since the twins were born."

"Yes, you can call and see if she'd like to come. I'm not the one with the great ideas, it's you!"

Saturday arrived, and Dad decided they would leave at ten o'clock. Mom made sure the twins had a morning nap and were fed before it was time to go. "We can ride together in our new van!" Mitch exclaimed.

It only took a minute to get to Grandma Clifton's. Dad pulled into Grandma Clifton's driveway and turned off the engine. Grandma Clifton was waiting on her front porch. Max opened the van door and helped her in. "This is such a delightful treat," Grandma Clifton bubbled. "I haven't been to the nursing home for a while now; thank you for asking me to come along."

A happy coo came from the seat behind Grandma Clifton. "Which baby is that?" she wondered.

"Melissa. We're delighted to have you," Mom turned around and squeezed Grandma Clifton's hand.

At the nursing home, Dad carried Melissa, and Mom situated Moses in the sling. "I like Melissa's headband." Grandma Clifton patted the baby's soft head.

"Mollie enjoys keeping headbands on Melissa," Dad said. "At first, Melissa didn't seem to notice, but as she's grown, she has begun to pull them off sometimes."

Miss Iva, the nursing home receptionist, was at the front desk. "The Moodys! What a surprise to see you." She gasped when she noticed the twins. "You had two babies?" Miss Iva was shocked. "You didn't look that big to me last time I saw you!"

"Yes, twin blessings," Mom smiled. "They were born early in March."

"The residents will love them. What are their names?"

"Melissa Joy and Moses Uriah."

"More 'M' names, keeping up the family tradition. Mr. Moody, I can't believe the timing of your visit today because our activities' director would like to talk with you about something. She's not usually in on Saturdays, but she's here today. I'll page her. Go ahead and visit; she'll find you. Ola Mae, it's good to see you!" She stood up and hugged the elderly lady. "How are you feeling?"

"I'm counting my blessings."

The family walked around, chatting with the residents. One lady, who introduced herself as Nellie, was moved to tears by the twins. "I haven't seen a baby for years! I had a set of twins when I was twenty-four, and they live far away right now. Seeing Moses and Melissa brings back a truckload of memories."

"They are sweet babies," Mom kissed Moses.

"You must be the Moodys," an enthusiastic voice greeted them. Mitch turned around and saw a dark-skinned lady who appeared to be in her early fifties, with curly black hair and a smile like he'd never seen.

"I'm Jennifer, the activities' director," she shook all of their hands. "I'm so glad to meet you! Iva's been telling me about your family."

They talked for a few minutes, until Jennifer said, "I have a request. Iva told me you are Christians and that you regularly come to visit our residents. I feel we have a great need here that isn't being fulfilled at this point. I have been praying about it and seeking the Lord for a solution. Here is the problem: we don't have a Christian church service on Sundays. I know it's important to some of the residents to be able to go to church. They have been going to church most, if not all, of their lives. Others are not saved, and these are the final days they have to receive Jesus as their Saviour. Delaware Heights has been without a Christian church service for three years. It is very difficult to find someone who will come in every week for church. Often churches are willing to have a monthly service at the nursing home but not weekly. I wondered if your family might consider spearheading a weekly church service here."

It took a moment before it dawned on Dad what she was asking. "Hmmmm. I have never considered anything like that before."

"I'd be blessed if you would at least think it over and pray about it. We really need a service every Sunday, not just once a month. I'm a Christian, and my heart has been grieved because we badly need a time of worship for our residents. I've tried asking other people, and no one will do it."

"We will definitely pray about it. When do you need to know by?"

"Anytime. I'll be patient." Jennifer shook their hands again before leaving.

The next day, after church, Dad asked Pastor Thompson if they could take a few minutes of his time. "Sure," he agreed. "Let's step into my office. Max and Mitch, why don't you grab a few chairs from the foyer and carry them in here so we'll have enough for the whole family?"

They all gathered into Pastor Thompson's small, cozy office. Dad began right away. "I received an unusual request yesterday while we were visiting the nursing home. I can't get it off my mind, and I've been praying about it ever since."

Pastor Thompson smiled. "You have my attention. What was the request?"

"Do you know the nursing home near our house?"

"Yes. I've been there quite a few times."

"Our family stopped in yesterday to share our twins with the residents. While we were there the activities' director asked if we'd consider having a weekly Sunday morning church service. I guess they haven't had a regular Christian service for three years! I've begun praying about it and wanted to know what you might think."

Pastor Thompson didn't hesitate. "I like it. That's what ministry, service, and outreach is all about. It isn't just within these four walls. What an opportunity the Lord is giving to your family. I'll do everything I can to support you. We'll want to find at least one other family who can help. I know just the one! I can't believe we didn't think of this earlier!"

Two evenings later, the twins were eleven weeks old. The family had finished devotions and were sitting near Moses and Melissa, who were lying on a blanket. "Our twins are getting so big," Mom exclaimed. "It seems just yesterday they were newborns."

"I wonder if Melissa's going to have blonde hair," Mollie patted a small tuft of hair.

"She might," Mom agreed.

A short knock was heard. "Hello!" Grandpa surprised the whole family, as he stepped in the front door, with Grandma close behind. "We decided to pop in for a short visit."

"We're glad to have you," Dad encouraged.

"Grandpa," Mitch had something on his mind. "Did you see the house sold next door? It wasn't for sale very long, and there is a sold sign on it. When Dad can catch the guy outside, he's going to ask him who bought the place. I hope we have good neighbors."

"You will," Grandpa said.

"Why, have you talked to the man?" Mitch was curious.

"No, but *we* bought the house, and we're planning to be the best neighbors you've ever had!"

Amazement filled the family's faces. Max was the first to speak. "Grandpa!!! Are you serious?! I can't believe it! What made you decide to leave your nice house in the country?"

Grandpa shook his head. "That wasn't hard. Grandma and I've been praying since the twins were born that a house would be for sale in this neighborhood! Your dad told me one morning at Bible study that if we ever wanted to live close by, you'd love it. So, with that in mind, the day after I saw the house on the market, I called the realtor. I could've signed papers on the house without looking at it, but we decided we should go ahead and tour it. That was a hard thing to do without you seeing us there. In fact, I had to wait until you were gone to the nursing home last Saturday to be able to do it. Grandma and I both knew we didn't need the size of house we have now, not to mention that with houses spread out, it would be hard to witness to our neighbors. Also, we wanted to be closer to you."

Dad beamed. "This will be such a blessing."

"I agree," Max said.

"Praise Jesus!" Mom's face was radiant. "Oh, praise Jesus for a wonderful family!"

"You will," Grandpa said.

The Moody Series Continues: Check out www.Titus2.com for the sequels that are available.

Spring with the Moodys
Not All Fiction!

Baby Traditions—I always looked forward to when a new baby joined our family, although we never had the double blessing of twins. My mom liked to have clean windows before a baby was born. After the baby was born, we children tried to make Mom feel special by taking care of her. We prepared her favorite foods. We also worked hard to keep the house clean and picked up while she was resting. Making phone calls to relatives and friends was also a highlight! It was a tradition to design a sign announcing the birth and attach the sign to the mailbox.

Baby Names—Baby names were a fun topic of conversation in our home during Mom's pregnancies, but Dad and Mom always chose the final name. In the not-too-distant past, Dad came to like the name "Uriah," but we never had a chance to use it for a baby who lived. We named a baby that was miscarried Joshua Uriah.

Grandparents—Our grandparents live right next door to us, which is a big blessing! The Lord gave the idea to have the Moodys' grandparents live next door as I was writing the book.

Church—Our family meets in a local nursing home for Sunday morning church services. Yes, that IS our church, and we love it! For more information about our church ministry, please visit: www.FamiliesforJesus.com

Witnessing—We are greatly indebted to Mr. Ray Comfort and his ministry, Living Waters, for learning how to more effectively witness, especially using the "Good Person" test. To see a list of tracts we prefer to use, please visit: www.FamiliesforJesus.com

Our Other Resources

Please see the following pages for information on the other books and audios my family offers.

Websites

www.Titus2.com   www.HomeschooleCards.com

www.ChorePacks.com   www.PreparingSons.com

www.FamiliesforJesus.com   www.PreparingDaughters.com

Feed My Sheep

A Practical Guide to Daily Family Bible Time
by Steve Maxwell
(More audio resources on page 208.)

Tried them and failed? Never tried because you knew it would be too big of a battle? No time for them even if you wanted to? Do any of these questions describe your experience with family Bible time? This two CD set is highly motivational and practical.

In the first CD, Steve Maxwell gives practical advice for achieving success with family Bible time. He reveals the secret that he guarantees will work

The second CD will help you gain ideas on how simple it is to implement a family Bible time as you join the Maxwell family for two of theirs. You'll feel like you're right at home with Steve as you listen to him lead his family in their time in the Word. You will see how easy it is to lead your family in the most important time of the day.

Join Steve, father of eight, as he shares about the Maxwells' favorite part of their day. We pray you'll come away with an excitement for the daily feeding of your family from God's Word!

To order or for information visit: www.Titus2.com.
Or call: (913) 772-0392.

The Moody Family Series

Summer (#1), Autumn (#2), Winter (#3), Spring (this book, #4), Summer Days (#5), and Autumn Days (#6, Available March 2011)

by Sarah Maxwell

Often parents are concerned about negative examples and role models in books their children are reading. One goal in writing the Moody Series was to eliminate those kinds of examples replacing them with positive, godly ones.

In the books, you'll find the Moodys helping a widowed neighbor, starting small businesses for the children, enjoying a fun night, training their new puppy, homeschooling, Mom experiencing morning sickness, and much more! Woven throughout the books is the Moodys' love for the Lord and their enjoyment of time together. Children (parents too!) will relate to the Moodys—they'll come away challenged and encouraged.

"My six-year-old son asked Jesus into his heart while we were reading Autumn with the Moodys. *These books are wonderful, heart-warming Christian reading. The Moodys will always have a special place in our hearts!" A mom*

"At last, a Christian book series that is engaging and encourages my children to love Jesus more and bless their family and friends." A mom

"We have been reading your Moody family series aloud for the last week, and my children cannot get enough." A mom

To order or for information visit: www.Titus2.com.
Or call: (913) 772-0392.

Managers of Their Homes

A Practical Guide to Daily Scheduling for Christian Homeschool Families

by Steven and Teri Maxwell

A homeschool mother's greatest challenge may be "getting it all done." *Managers of Their Homes* offers solutions! Responses by families who have read *Managers of Their Homes* and utilized the Scheduling Kit indicate the almost unbelievable improvements they have realized.

Step-by-step instructions and a unique Scheduling Kit make the setting up of a daily schedule easily achievable for any homeschooling family. Who wouldn't like to accomplish more and have time left over?

How does one schedule school time? Are you struggling with keeping up in areas such as laundry, dishes, or housekeeping? Do you feel stressed over the busyness of your days or not accomplishing all you want? It doesn't matter whether you have one child or twelve, this book will help you to plan your daily schedule.

Managers of Their Homes sets a firm biblical foundation for scheduling, in addition to discussing scheduling's numerous benefits. Chapter after chapter is filled with practical suggestions for efficient, workable ways to schedule a homeschooling family's days. Thirty real-life schedules in the Appendix give valuable insight into creating a personalized schedule. Also included is a special chapter by Steve for homeschool dads.

"My schedule has given me back my sanity!! I can't believe the way my life has changed since implementing a schedule." Tracy

"Making and using a schedule has helped me, and there were people who thought I was hopeless!" Sheri

"I had read almost every organizational book there was, and I still couldn't get to where I wanted to be until I applied this method!" Corrie

To order or for information visit: www.Titus2.com.
Or call: (913) 772-0392.

Managers of Their Chores

A Practical Guide to Children's Chores

by Steven and Teri Maxwell

In the same way that *Managers of Their Homes* helped tens of thousands of moms "get it all done," *Managers of Their Chores* helps families conquer the chore battle. The book and included ChorePack system have the potential to revolutionize the way your family accomplishes chores. Whether you are chore challenged or a seasoned chore warrior, you will gain motivation and loads of practical advice on implementing a stress-free chore system.

Managers of Their Chores comes with all the ChorePack materials needed for four children, including ChorePacks, chore card paper, and a ChorePack holder. In the appendix of the book, you will find a chore library with more than 180 chores listed, forms for photocopying, and sample chore assignments from eight families.

Use *Managers of Their Chores* to help your family achieve a chore system that is as stress free as possible. This book puts tools into parents' hands that will allow them to be successful in a chore system with their children. From preschoolers to teens, each person can be a contributing member of the family while gaining lifelong personal benefits that prepare him for life.

"I can't believe how much time we have gained in our days now that we have our ChorePack system in place." A mom

"Its simplicity and ease of use encouraged independence and accountability at a young age." A mom

"It gave you visuals, explained the whys, needs, and benefits of chores, plus giving a system for implementing them. The book walked you through the process very clearly one step at a time with explanation of what to do and why." A mom

To order or for information visit: www.Titus2.com.
Or call: (913) 772-0392.

Managers of Their Schools

A Practical Guide to Homeschooling

by Steven and Teri Maxwell

Have you ever wanted to sit down with an experienced homeschooling couple and ask them every question you could think of about homeschooling? *Managers of Their Schools: A Practical Guide to Homeschooling* is the next best thing. With eight children and twenty-three years as a homeschooling family, the Maxwells share their answers to the questions they are frequently asked.

This book is filled with practical information regarding how one family homeschools, what they use, why they do what they do, and how it all works for them. Steve and Teri set down the details of homeschooling in a real-life family, from how they make curricula decisions to whether their children take tests.

After spending their first twelve years searching for a homeschool method that met their Scriptural and educational criteria, they finally began using Christian textbooks and have never wanted to change direction again. In this book, Steve and Teri share the benefits their family has gained from using textbooks, and they refute the reasons many will say homeschoolers should not use textbooks.

There is a chapter written by four of the adult Maxwell children sharing some of their homeschool thoughts, particularly with regard to using Christian textbooks. The appendix of *Managers of Their Schools* includes ten of the Maxwell's school schedules, several assignment sheets, a listing of the school curricula and resources the Maxwells personally use, plus coupon codes for discounts on some of them.

Whether or not you use the same method to home educate as the Maxwells, you will find a wealth of tried-and-true, daily-life homeschool information. Make your homeschooling journey that much easier, more efficient, and more joyful by learning from a family who has already walked the path.

"I have learned so much from the book. The time I will save in planning for this school year is astronomical!" A mom

To order or for information visit: www.Titus2.com.
Or call: (913) 772-0392.

Keeping Our Children's Hearts

Our Vital Priority

By Steven and Teri Maxwell

Written for parents of young children to teenagers, this book shares the joys and outcomes of our vital priority—keeping our children's hearts. Rebellion and immorality are common among teens even within the Christian community. Does Scripture offer any path of hope for more than this for our children? What can parents do to direct their children toward godliness rather than worldliness? When does this process begin? What is the cost?

Steve and Teri Maxwell believe the key factors in raising children in the nurture and admonition of the Lord (Ephesians 6:4) are whether or not the parents have their children's hearts and what they are doing with those hearts. *Keeping Our Children's Hearts* offers direction and encouragement on this critically important topic.

Included in this book is a chapter co-authored by three of the adult Maxwell children concerning their thoughts, feelings, experiences, and outcomes of growing up in a home where their parents wanted to keep their hearts. There are also questions at the end of each chapter, which are thought provoking and helpful.

"The most complete and most balanced book I have read on how to raise children who won't rebel!" Dr. S. M. Davis

"This book is making me rethink what my purpose as a Christian, mother, and homeschooler should be." A mom

"The Scripture and its experiential application was encouraging and refreshing." A dad

"It truly is my top child rearing book now. You have brought together all the issues we have been striving to understand and achievements we hope to make with our children." A mom

**To order or for information visit: www.Titus2.com.
Or call: (913) 772-0392.**

Homeschooling with a Meek and Quiet Spirit

by Teri Maxwell

The desire of a homeschooling mother's heart is to have a meek and quiet spirit instead of discouragement, fear, and anger.

Because Teri Maxwell, a mother of eight, has walked the homeschooling path since 1985, she knows first-hand the struggle for a meek and quiet spirit. The memories from her early homeschooling years of often being worried and angry rather than having a meek and quiet spirit are not what she would like them to be.

Will your journey toward a meek and quiet spirit be completed upon finding the perfect spelling curriculum or deciding which chores your child should be doing? Perhaps the answer lies on a different path.

In these pages, Teri offers practical insights into gaining a meek and quiet spirit that any mom can apply to her individual circumstances. She transparently shares the struggles God has brought her through and what He has shown her during these many homeschooling years.

As you read *Homeschooling with a Meek and Quiet Spirit,* you will discover the heart issues that will gently lead you to a meek and quiet spirit. Come along and join Teri as you seek the Lord to homeschool with a meek and quiet spirit!

A study guide is also available.

"This is one of the best, most helpful, encouraging, and empathetic books I've read during my 5 years of homeschooling." A mom

"I wish all moms, regardless of their school choice, could read Homeschooling with a Meek and Quiet Spirit." *Kathy*

"It is not just for homeschooling moms, but any mom who wants to be the best mom she can be. It was challenging, enlightening, and encouraging." A mom

To order or for information visit: www.Titus2.com.
Or call: (913) 772-0392.

Redeeming the Time

A Practical Guide to a Christian Man's Time Management

by Steven Maxwell

Most men today would say that they are under time pressure. In the midst of their busyness, there are key aspects of their daily lives that suffer such as their relationships with the Lord, with their wives, and with their children. They aren't keeping up with their normal responsibilities. They are tired, stressed, and struggling.

Author, Titus2.com ministry founder, engineer, and CEO of two small businesses, Steve Maxwell has much experience in time management. He shares Biblical truths that will allow a man to gain control over the time pressures that he is facing. Steve discusses practical aspects of time management that put a man on a path to being able to keep up with the various demands on his time. In this book you will learn how it is possible to go from pressure, chaos, and stress to peace, order, and productivity.

"After reading this book, I have a better idea and understanding of what God expects from me as the DAD!" A dad

"The material covered in this book is sorely needed for followers of Christ." A dad

"It is a wonderful book. It has really changed my life. I've got more time than I ever thought I would have." A dad

"Touches issues in a man's life that are often in disrepair." A dad

"Excellent examples and personal experiences." A dad

"This book will help you take control of the time the Lord gave you, redeeming it for treasures that will be timeless." A dad

Redeeming the Time is available in paperback or unabridged audiobook.

To order or for information visit: www.Titus2.com.
Or call: (913) 772-0392.

Preparing Sons

to Provide for a Single-Income Family

By Steven Maxwell

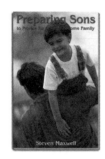

In today's world of two-income families, preparing a son to provide for a single-income family seems an overwhelming task. Christian parents will find it helpful to have a purpose and plan as they raise sons who will one day be responsible for supporting a family.

Steve Maxwell presents the groundwork for preparing your son to be a wage-earning adult. He gives practical suggestions and direction to parents for working with their sons from preschool age all the way to adulthood. You will be challenged to evaluate your own life and the example you are setting for your son.

As the father of eight children, six of them now wage-earning adults, Steve has gained valuable experience he openly shares with other parents. Learn these principles from a dad whose twenty-four-year-old homeschooled son purchased a home debt free a year before his marriage, and whose second son has done the same. Steve explains how it is possible for parents, with a willing commitment, to properly prepare their sons to provide for a single-income family.

"You are dealing with topics that no one I know of has dealt with as thoroughly and practically as you have." Dr. S. M. Davis

"Preparing Sons *was a big blessing to my husband. All you ladies should get a copy for your husband and every church library needs one." Shelly*

"I highly recommend the book for those of you who have not read it. I really appreciate all the obvious prayer, effort, and experience that went into making this book. The Lord is using it for His Glory in our family." Les

Preparing Sons *is available in paperback or unabridged audiobook.*

To order or for information visit: www.Titus2.com.
Or call: (913) 772-0392.

Just Around the Corner

Encouragement and Challenge for Christian Dads and Moms, Volumes 1 and 2 (Volume 3 Coming Soon!)

By Steven and Teri Maxwell

Just Around the Corner (Volumes 1 and 2) is a compilation of Steve and Teri Maxwell's monthly Dad's and Mom's Corners. These articles are written to help and challenge Christian parents, many of whom may not have grown up with godly role models.

Are you content with the way things are in your family? Do you feel like you are running on a treadmill? Do you want to have sweet relationships with your children as they are growing up and not experience the heartache of rebellion and immorality? Are you looking for practical guidance to a deeper family walk with Jesus Christ? These are a few of the topics addressed in these indexed books.

Steve's writing will challenge a dad in his role as the spiritual head of the family. Teri's writing addresses many aspects of daily life that often frustrate or discourage a mom.

Authored by the parents of eight children, the volumes provide encouragement that dads and moms are seeking for their personal walks with the Lord Jesus, their roles as husbands and wives, and the raising of their children. Through *Just Around the Corner*, the Maxwells want to show you ways—some of which you may never have imagined—that God can set your family on a spiritual journey.

"Just Around the Corner *has helped me to regain my focus and carry on to what God has called me to do.*" Michelle

To order or for information visit: www.Titus2.com.
Or call: (913) 772-0392.